Twice the Talent

by Belle Payton

Simon Spotlight

New York London Toronto Sydney New Delhi

SIMON SPOTLIGHT
An imprint of Simon & Schuster Children's Publishing Division
1230 Avenue of the Americas, New York, New York 10020
This Simon Spotlight edition January 2016
Text by Tracey West
Cover art by Anthony VanArsdale
© 2016 by Simon & Schuster, Inc.
All rights reserved, including the right of reproduction in whole or in part in any form.
SIMON SPOTLIGHT and colophon are registered trademarks of
Simon & Schuster, Inc.
For information about special discounts for bulk purchases, please
contact Simon & Schuster Special Sales at 1-866-506-1949 or
business@simonandschuster.com.
Designed by Ciara Gay
The text of this book was set in Garamond.
Manufactured in the United States of America 1215 OFF
10 9 8 7 6 5 4 3 2 1
ISBN 978-1-4814-5264-9 (hc)
ISBN 978-1-4814-5263-2 (pbk)
ISBN 978-1-4814-5265-6 (eBook)
Library of Congress Catalog Card Number 2015938113

CHAPTER ONE

"So it really happened just like that?" Alex Sackett asked.

"Absolutely," answered Charlotte Huang. "Mom was like, this kitchen renovation is driving me crazy, I just can't take it anymore, and the next thing I knew we were on a plane to the Bahamas."

"That sounds amazing," said Rosa Navarro, a dreamy look in her brown eyes.

It was a Tuesday afternoon, Christmas break was over, and Alex and her friends Charlotte, Rosa, Emily, Lindsey, and Annelise were hanging out at Emily's house. They had piled into Emily's cozy bedroom. Alex sat on the floor, clutching a throw pillow.

Sometimes it was hard to believe that she and her family had only moved to Ashland, Texas, a few months ago. It hadn't been easy to leave her life and friends in Boston behind—but here she was, with all new friends, laughing and talking like she'd known them forever.

"What's amazing is your tan, Charlotte," said Annelise. "I get so pale during the winter."

"Not to mention freezing," said Lindsey with a shiver. "I'd love to be on a sunny beach right now."

Alex held back a smile. It was forty-nine degrees out, which was chilly for Texas, but downright balmy for a winter day in Boston.

Emily, the girl in the group Alex felt closest to, noticed her amused expression.

"I bet this is beach weather in Boston, right, Alex?" she teased.

"Exactly," said Alex, playing along. "Back home everyone's wearing flip-flops and building snow castles by the ocean."

"Ooh, we built this fabulous sand castle at the beach by our hotel," said Charlotte, scrolling through her phone to find the photos. "Mom hired a sand castle architect, and he helped us. It had, like, twenty towers and a stable and everything."

Alex raised an eyebrow. "Is there really such a thing as a sand castle architect?" she asked. Although as soon as she asked the question, she knew she shouldn't have been surprised. Charlotte's family had two housekeepers and a driver. Hiring someone to help build your sand castle was probably no big deal.

"Yeah, he worked with the hotel," Charlotte replied, and then she frowned. "I can't find it! Oh, wait, here's that shot from the Christmas party!"

Everyone gathered around Charlotte to look, even though they all had tons of photos from the party on their phones. They'd held an Ugly Sweater party on the Saturday after Christmas, and it had probably been Alex's best night in Ashland so far.

The photo on Charlotte's screen was a group selfie of everyone in their ugly sweaters, mugging for the camera. There was Alex, laughing with her arm around her twin sister, Ava. They looked identical except for Alex's long, wavy hair and Ava's shorter, sporty haircut.

Next to Alex was Emily, sticking her tongue out, and Lindsey, who was posing like a supermodel.

There were boys in the photo too, but the one who caught Alex's eye was Corey O'Sullivan. He wore a silly grin on his face and a Santa hat on top of his red hair.

"That was such a fun night," said Rosa. "Although I'm glad I won't have to wear that ugly sweater ever again!"

"The sweaters are what made it a fun night," Emily pointed out.

"And the Secret Santa exchange," added Annelise.

Lindsey got a mischievous twinkle in her eyes. "That was a sweet gift that Corey gave you, Alex," she said quietly. "You know, you never told me if you and Corey used that mistletoe."

Alex felt her face get hot, and she knew she must be bright red. She and Corey had almost kissed that night, under the falling snow, but she hadn't told anybody about it—not even Ava. She wasn't about to tell anyone in this room.

Part of the reason was that everything with Corey was super complicated. She had developed a crush on him right away when she first met him, but then she learned that Lindsey liked him too, so she backed off. Corey and Lindsey went out, but broke up. Then Lindsey started liking Johnny Morton, an eighth grader. That led to the Christmas party, where she gave Alex mistletoe and told her she should go talk to Corey.

And Alex had talked to Corey, outside, and they almost kissed—until the snow started to fall, which didn't happen too often in Texas. Everyone had streamed outside, and the moment was over. But it had still been a magical moment, and it had been hers—just hers and Corey's.

"Mistletoe? What about Alex and Corey and mistletoe?" Annelise asked eagerly.

"Hey, didn't we come here so that you guys could work on your Variety Show routine?" Alex asked, trying to change the subject.

Her ploy worked. "That's right!" Emily said, jumping up off her bed. "The show is only three weeks away and we've barely started practicing."

"Or working on our costumes," said Rosa. "We've got to think of something that will go with the Wild West theme."

"So what are you guys doing?" asked Alex. The Variety Show seemed to be a big deal at Ashland Middle School. It was just about all anyone could talk about now that the holidays were over.

Annelise smiled. "We're going to do a dance, like we did last year. You should dance with us!"

"Come on, you know I have two left feet," Alex said. "Besides, as student council president I volunteered to work backstage."

"That makes sense. I can just see you with a clipboard, organizing everybody back there. It can get pretty hectic," Emily remarked.

Lindsey shook her head. "You could still dance with us. It's a pretty easy dance. Charlotte's new, and she picked it up right away. Here, I'll show you."

Lindsey jumped up and kicked a pillow out of her way. Then she played a song on her phone. It was a country song that Alex had never heard before, something about a broken heart.

Lindsey started moving her hips from side to side and tracing a heart in the air with her fingers. Emily, Rosa, Charlotte, and Annelise joined her. It was close quarters and the girls kept bumping into one another. They looked a little stiff, and frankly, Alex thought, pretty silly.

"See how easy it is?" Lindsey asked. "Anytime you hear the word 'heart,' you just go like this." She traced a heart in the air again.

"Wow, that looks way too complicated," Alex

fibbed. "Now that I've seen it, I know I would just make a fool out of myself up there. And I am trying very hard not to commit myself to too many activities anymore. But I promise that I will be cheering you on backstage."

"Aw, it's not *that* complicated," Lindsey protested.

"If I can do it, you can do it!" Charlotte said, as she bumped into Rosa.

Alex glanced at the clock on Emily's nightstand. Four o'clock. She'd almost forgotten.

"Sorry, I have to get to Ava's game," she said, grabbing her backpack. "But you guys look great!"

Alex hurried out of the room, relieved to be spared from joining the dance routine.

Sometimes having a twin sister came in handy!

CHAPTER TWO

The sound of Coach Rader's whistle rang through the Ashland Middle School gym.

"All right, Cubs! Time to stretch!" he called out.

Ava Sackett ran onto the basketball court with the rest of her teammates. She lined up with the others while her friend Callie Wagner—who had recently been made team captain—jogged forward to lead them in stretches.

As Ava stretched, she started to feel the energy flow through her body. She loved that excitement that built up inside her just before a game. It was almost the same feeling she got when she had played football with the Tiger Cubs in the fall.

On the football team, she had the added pressure of being the only girl on the boys' team. But she also had the confidence that arose from having played football pretty much ever since she could walk. That came with the territory when your dad was a football coach, although her twin sister, Alex, couldn't explain the difference between a running back and a wide receiver.

Here on the basketball team, Ava didn't have to worry about standing out as the only girl. But while she had shot many casual games of hoops in parks with her friends, she had never played basketball on a school team before.

As she stretched, she glanced over at the other side of the court, where the girls on the Midvale Mustangs were warming up in their brown-and-white uniforms.

They look so tall! Ava thought, as nervousness about the game crept in.

Coach Rader's whistle blared again. He was also Ava's English teacher, and she was grateful he didn't use his whistle in class.

"All right! Time for drills! Just like we did at practice!" Coach called out.

The girls jogged into position.

"We've got twenty minutes to warm up before each game, and we're going to make the most of it," Coach Rader had explained at the last practice. Then he'd outlined their warm-up routine.

Ava and four other girls practiced dribbling on the left side of the court. On the right side, two girls practiced passing in a zigzag pattern up and down the half-court. In the center, three players took turns shooting and catching rebounds.

"Go, Ava!" someone in the stands yelled, and Ava looked up to see her best friend, Kylie McClaire, holding up a sign that said the same thing. Kylie had even threaded blue and orange beads—the Tiger Cubs colors—into her braided hair.

Ava grinned. Kylie didn't even really like sports, but she had shown up to every football game Ava had ever played in, and now, here she was at Ava's first basketball game. Ava felt lucky to have made such a good friend so soon after moving to Ashland.

Ava's mom and dad sat behind Kylie and gave her a wave.

"Ava, figure eights!" Madison Jackson hissed at her, and Ava realized she had lost focus during the drill. She started dribbling the ball between her legs, directing it left and then right to make a figure-eight pattern as she dribbled.

Convincing her parents to let her join the basketball team hadn't been easy. Shortly after they'd moved to Ashland, Ava had been diagnosed with ADHD. She'd been assigned to a learning specialist at school, which helped. And a sophomore named Luke, who was friends with her older brother, Tommy, had started tutoring her at night, which had been great—until she realized that half the basketball practices were at night because other teams needed the gym in the afternoon.

Ava's parents were worried that the nighttime practices would interfere with her study schedule, but Ava had convinced them that playing basketball would actually help her get good grades, not hurt her. And so far, Ava had been right. She was practicing hard and getting decent grades too. Now she just had to prove that it was all worth it—right here on the court.

Tweeeeeeeet! At the sound of the whistle, Ava and Madison ran across the court to begin zigzag passes. Their sneakers pounded in rhythm as they moved up and down the half-court, passing the ball back and forth to each other.

Ava was facing the bleachers, so as she caught the ball from Madison, she saw her twin sister Alex enter the gym and climb up to meet their parents.

Tweeeeeeet! Ava and Madison moved to the basket, where they were joined by a tall blond girl named Tamara whom Ava didn't know very well. Ava knew Tamara was related to Andy and PJ and was wondering if she was mean like them when Madison jogged to the foul line and shot the ball.

Swoosh! Ava caught the rebound and switched places with Madison, taking her turn to shoot.

Another *swoosh!* Ava grinned.

I just hope the game goes this well! Ava thought, but the warm-up had helped get rid of her nervousness. She had practiced hard for this. She had done the impossible and convinced her parents to let her play. She was ready!

Tweeeet! "All right, Cubs! Time to huddle!" Coach Rader called out.

In the stands, Alex watched her sister jog off the court and get into a tight circle with the other girls on her team.

"This is so exciting!" Alex blurted out to her parents. She knew how much playing basketball meant to Ava and could only imagine how her sister felt right now.

Her father nodded. "I'm excited for your sister too," said Coach. "Ava has worked so hard for this."

Five girls from each team came out onto the court, and Alex noticed that Ava was one of them. Callie stood in the center circle, with Ava and Madison on either side of her.

"What does it mean that Ava is up front like that?" Alex asked.

"The coach is starting Ava as a forward," her mom explained. "Madison is a forward too, and Callie is the center. And the two girls behind them are guards."

"That's Tamara and Tessa," Alex said, recognizing them. "So, they're like the defense?"

"Not really," her mom said. "They actually handle the ball and shoot the most."

Alex took out her phone and typed the positions in her notes. She wasn't super interested in basketball, but she hated being left out of the conversation at dinnertime, and she had a feeling that basketball would be a popular topic for the next few weeks.

The referee blew his whistle and tossed the ball in the air between the team's two centers. The Mustangs' center jumped up and pushed the ball forward, but the pass went wild and Tessa grabbed it. She dribbled forward and passed it to Ava, who caught it. Ava took it down the middle of the court and passed it to Callie, who was open right under the basket. Callie jumped up, shot, and scored!

Two points appeared on the scoreboard, and the Tiger Cubs fans in the bleachers let out a cheer. Alex cheered louder than anybody.

There was something really fun about watching Ava play basketball. When she played on the football team, there was always that underlying tension, knowing that many people in the stands were wondering the same thing: Was Ava as good as the boys? Would she get hurt?

But here, on the basketball court, that pressure was off.

Alex thought about how she had been running for class president at the same time Ava was causing a stir by trying out for the football team. *I'm so happy basketball season is going to be much less stressful than football season—for both of us!* she mused.

On the court, Ava grinned and slapped Callie's hand. The Mustangs' center passed the ball to one of the forwards, who lobbed a long pass down the court to one of the open Mustang guards. Ava charged down the court just as the guard lost her grip on the pass and the ball bounced away. Ava retrieved it and dribbled it back down the court. She saw Madison open and passed the ball to her.

Madison caught it, but two Mustangs immediately surrounded her. Trapped, she jumped up and took a shot, but it fell just short of the basket.

Callie grabbed it and quickly shot it at Ava, who caught it and made the shot from the right corner.

Swoosh! The ball sailed through the net.

"Go, Ava!" cheered Kylie from the stands.

"Yaaay, Ava!" yelled Alex.

The Tiger Cubs scored once more during the first quarter, and the Mustangs scored again to make the score 6–2, Cubs, when the quarter ended. Coach Rader benched Ava and the four other girls on the court and put in five different members of the team.

"Looking good out there," Coach Rader said to the starters on the bench, and Ava could feel herself beaming with pride. The game was off to a great start!

The Cubs kept their lead in the second quarter, which ended 10–5 after one of the Mustangs made an impossible basket from past the three-point line. Otherwise, their defense kept making the mistake of converging around the player who had the ball while leaving other players open.

Coach Rader put Ava, Callie, Madison, Tessa, and Tamara back in for the third quarter. By then the Mustangs seemed to have figured out their defensive problem, and only Madison was able to score. The quarter ended 12–9—too close for comfort.

The girls came back to the sidelines.

"Their defense is getting better, but they're still clumping up under the basket," he told the girls. "Ava and Madison, stay close to the sidelines if you can, and try to shoot from there."

Ava and Madison nodded, and the girls jogged back onto the court. Callie got control of the ball, but one of the Mustangs stole it from her. She drove down the court and made a successful layup.

The scoreboard now read HOME 12, GUEST 11, and Ava started to feel nervous for the first time.

"Ava!" she heard Madison cry out, and Ava realized she had lost focus for a second—long enough for one of the Mustangs to bat the ball out of Madison's hands. She passed it down the court to her teammate, who took a shot and missed. Ava ran up to catch the rebound. Ava passed it to Callie, who passed it to Madison, but Madison missed her shot too.

For the next seven minutes it seemed like neither team could score. Then one of the Mustangs fumbled a pass, and Tamara recovered it and passed it to Ava.

Stay close to the sidelines, Coach Rader had said, and Ava stuck close to the left side of the court. One of the Mustangs came toward her, and Ava quickly looked to see if anyone was open—but nobody was. In the three seconds before the Mustang player reached her, she jumped up and took a shot, twisting her body to the right to avoid colliding with the Mustang.

She watched the ball bounce off the backboard and sink right into the net—and then she landed. Hard.

CHAPTER THREE

Buzzzzzzzzzzz!

The final buzzer rang, and a cheer went up from the stands.

"We won!" Madison cried, running up to hug her, and Ava winced. When she'd landed, she'd felt her right ankle buckle underneath her and a shot of pain jolt through her body. The victory cheers rang hollow in her ears as the pain in her ankle made her head feel fuzzy.

Then the Cubs lined up to shake hands with the Mustangs, and Ava joined them, trying not to limp. Coach Rader approached her.

"Ava, I saw you come down hard on that ankle," he said. "How's it feeling?"

"Fine, Coach," Ava lied. She had just played her first game of basketball and loved it. There was no way she was admitting that her ankle hurt—what if it was really messed up, and she was out for the season? That would be so unfair!

She gritted her teeth and headed to the locker room without limping the whole way, but it was extremely painful. When she finished changing, she found her family waiting in the gym for her.

"Great game!" Alex cried, hugging her. "I think I might like watching basketball more than football."

Mrs. Sackett was concerned. "Ave, it looked like you twisted your ankle when you took that last shot."

"I'm fine," Ava insisted.

Her father looked up from his phone. "Uncle Scott just texted. He's making a special sweet and spicy tofu for dinner to celebrate."

"Oh, boy," said Ava, and she and her dad exchanged sympathetic looks. While they had both gotten used to Uncle Scott's cooking since he moved in, neither of them would choose tofu as their way to celebrate Ava's big win.

Ava ignored her painful ankle all through

dinner and while she was doing her homework that night. But the next morning, her ankle was as purple as an eggplant and about the same size. When she stood up, she could barely put weight on it.

Alex was the first to see her as she made her way to the bathroom, clutching the wall for support.

"Oh no, Ave!" she cried, looking down at her twin's ankle. "Why didn't you say anything?"

"I didn't think it was that bad," Ava admitted. "And I don't want to be benched for the season. I'm sure it'll get better soon."

Alex shook her head. "Ava, you are being ridiculous," she told her sister. Then she marched right downstairs.

Ava cringed, and not from the pain in her ankle. She knew what would happen once her parents saw it.

She got dressed in jeans and a red T-shirt, but she couldn't even pull a sock over her ankle. She hobbled downstairs wearing only one sock.

Mrs. Sackett was already shaking her head. "Ava, let me see that ankle, please," she said firmly.

Ava sighed. "It's not that bad!"

Her mother gasped. "Ava, this is a serious injury! I am calling Dr. Rodriguez right now."

Ava glared at Alex. "Thanks for telling her!"

"She would have figured it out anyway when you tried to leave the house wearing only one shoe," Alex retorted, taking a bite of her cereal.

Uncle Scott came into the kitchen, yawning. His eyes got wide when he saw Ava's ankle.

"Whoa," he said. "I know someone who makes a tincture for sprains and strains. I'll give her a call."

"What she needs first is an X-ray," Mrs. Sackett said, sounding a little stressed. She didn't always have patience for her brother-in-law's way of doing things.

Mrs. Sackett called the doctor while Alex headed off to the bus stop. Ava moped around gloomily until nine o'clock, when her mom helped her into the car and drove her to see Dr. Rodriguez.

Dr. Rodriguez was nice enough, with serious brown eyes behind his glasses. But the visit to the doctor's office took forever. First he examined her ankle and decided to send Ava for an X-ray in another wing of the office building.

Then Ava and her mom had to wait while he looked at the film.

Finally he called them back into his office.

"What we have here is a pretty serious sprain," he said, and he held up a black fabric brace with Velcro straps. "You'll need to wear this for at least six weeks."

Six weeks! Ava felt like screaming. That was forever!

"Will she need crutches?" Mrs. Sackett asked.

"No," the doctor replied. "She can walk normally with the brace. This will protect her from further injuries."

Ava felt a surge of hope. "So can I play basketball with the brace on too?"

"Maybe, in about three weeks," Dr. Rodriguez answered.

This time Ava let out her wail. "Three weeks! But the season just started!"

Alex was walking to social studies class when she suddenly got a strange feeling that something was wrong with Ava. Like maybe her ankle was really hurt. That happened sometimes—she could feel when Ava was really upset or really happy, even if she wasn't nearby. Tommy called it their "freaky twin connection."

When she walked into the room, Emily, Lindsey, and Rosa were gathered around Lindsey's desk, talking. Emily noticed the strange look on Alex's face.

"Alex, is something wrong?" she asked.

"I'm sure it's nothing," Alex said. "I just have a weird feeling that something's not going to go well for Ava. It's our twin thing, I guess."

Lindsey's eyes got wide. "Ooh, your twin thing. So you're having a preignition, right?"

Alex knew that Lindsey was actually thinking of "precognition," but she didn't want to correct her friend. Then a boy's voice interrupted them.

"You mean precognition," Max Beedle said with a laugh. "The psychic ability to predict the future. Preignition would be like pre-starting your car or something. Not as impressive."

Alex smiled—Lindsey had made kind of a funny mistake. But Lindsey's cheeks were red, and she was glaring at Max. Alex looked at him. She didn't know him very well—no one seemed to, because he was quiet and mostly kept to himself. And although he was kind of cute, he was always a mess. His wavy brown hair wasn't combed, and today he was wearing a blue collared shirt that was half tucked in and half sticking out. Alex couldn't help noticing that he had on two different sweat socks: one black and one white.

And though he didn't talk much, when he did, he usually said something odd. Like he just had with Lindsey, who looked like she was about to snap at him. But the bell rang before she could.

"Good morning, class," said their teacher, Mrs. Bridges. "Today we're going to continue our discussion on the formation of democracy in America after the revolution."

She dimmed the lights in the class, and a presentation appeared on the screen behind her. Then she launched into her lecture.

After ten minutes, she turned up the lights.

"Max, can you please tell me one of the challenges that led to the Constitutional Convention?" she asked.

Her only response was the sound of a soft snore. Alex looked and saw that Max's head was down on his desk. He had fallen asleep—and it wasn't the first time he had done that in class. Several kids began to laugh.

"Max, am I interrupting your nap?" Mrs. Bridges asked loudly.

"Um, what?" Max asked groggily, lifting his head, and the class laughed again.

"I was asking if you could tell me one of the challenges that led to the Constitutional Convention," the teacher repeated.

Max frowned. "Um, like rights or something?"

Mrs. Bridges sighed. "Anybody else?"

Alex's hand shot up, and the teacher called on her.

"Economic struggles caused by the Articles of Confederation," she answered. Who didn't know that? *Poor Max must be really out of it,* Alex guessed.

"Correct, Alex, as always," said Mrs. Bridges. "Now, before the bell rings, I wanted to let you know we're going to be starting a new class project."

A few kids groaned, but the teacher ignored them.

"Your projects will be on the Bill of Rights," she went on. "I will be assigning students to work in pairs. Stay tuned!"

Alex looked across the room at Emily. Maybe they could be partners. Of course, Lindsey and

Rosa were in the class too, so Emily might want to pair up with one of them. That was the tough thing about joining an already established group of friends. Sometimes it was hard to know where she stood.

The class bell rang, and Alex gathered up her books. A few rows in front of her, Lindsey and Rosa were talking loudly.

"Maybe Max should go back to preschool. They have naptime there," Lindsey said.

"And what's with his hair?" Rosa wondered. "Does he use a rake to brush it?"

Max was still in the classroom, trying to shove a stack of messy papers back into his binder, and Alex knew he had heard the girls. His cheeks turned red and he bolted out of the room, the loose half of his shirt flapping behind him.

Lindsey has probably been waiting this whole class period to get back at Max for embarrassing her, Alex thought, *and Max gave her the perfect reason to make fun of him.* Alex felt sorry for him. She didn't think he'd really meant to embarrass Lindsey.

She thought about telling Lindsey that and decided not to. She had been trying so hard to be friends with her, and things had finally settled down once Lindsey stopped liking Corey. She didn't want to jeopardize that now.

She looked over at Emily, who had joined Lindsey and Rosa. Now they were talking about the Variety Show. That settled it. If Emily wasn't going to say anything to Lindsey, Alex wouldn't either.

Still, she felt uneasy as she headed to her next class—and not just because of Max. She still couldn't shake that feeling that something was wrong with Ava!

CHAPTER FOUR

"You know, if you ate an Ayurvedic diet like I do, you might heal a lot faster," Uncle Scott told Ava.

After coming back from the doctor's, Mrs. Sackett had instructed Ava to sit on the couch with her ankle raised. She had to keep an ice pack on it for twenty minutes at a time until the swelling went down. Moxy, the family's Australian shepherd, sat on the floor near Ava's feet, staring at the ice pack like it was a squirrel in a tree.

Ava was absently changing channels on the TV when Uncle Scott had walked in. He had moved into the Sackett household in December, out of a job and with no place to live. Some good had resulted from Uncle Scott moving in;

for one thing, he had helped Ava convince her parents that playing basketball was a good thing for her.

But the house was just big enough for five Sacketts, and sometimes it was stressful having Uncle Scott squeeze in. He slept in the study, and if he went to sleep early, the girls had to tiptoe around the house and couldn't turn the volume up on the TV.

"So, if I go totally Ayurvedic, I can't eat cheeseburgers, right?" Ava asked.

"Right," said Uncle Scott.

"And no onion rings?" Ava asked.

Uncle Scott shook his head. "No onion rings. But it'll be totally worth it, Ava. I promise."

Her uncle's dark eyes glittered with intensity when he talked about something he believed in—like recycling, or renewable sources of energy, or his specialized vegetarian diet.

"So, if I do this, can you guarantee I'll be back on the basketball court sooner?" Ava asked.

"Ava, there are no guarantees," Uncle Scott replied. "But it would be a smart thing to do."

Ava leaned back into the couch cushions. "If you can't guarantee it, forget it," she said crossly.

Uncle Scott put a sympathetic hand on her shoulder. "I know this is tough for you, Ava. I'm going to make a mix of calming music that I think will help your mood."

Alex came into the living room, carrying her backpack.

"Who needs to change their mood?" Alex asked.

"Ava's just feeling bummed out that she can't play basketball for three weeks," Uncle Scott reported, as he headed into the study.

"Three weeks!" Alex cried, plopping down on the couch next to Ava. "Oh, Ava, that's terrible. I had a feeling something was really wrong with your ankle. Is it broken?"

Ava shook her head. "Just a sprain. But I have to wear this stupid brace all the time, and even after three weeks the doctor says I have to wear the brace when I play!"

Alex looked thoughtful. "Well, a brace is a lot better than an itchy cast. It could be a lot worse."

"It could *not* be worse!" Ava protested. She knew she was being really crabby, but she couldn't help it. She was stuck on the couch with her leg in the air when she should be at basketball practice.

Mrs. Sackett came into the living room with a streak of gray clay on her arm. She was a potter, and she'd worked on some of her pieces at home today instead of going into a studio like she normally did. "How was your day, Alex?" she asked.

"Pretty good," Alex reported.

"Of course it was good," Ava said. "*She's* not stuck in a stupid leg brace with a stupid sprained ankle."

Alex looked at her mother and rolled her eyes.

"I saw that!" Ava cried.

Mrs. Sackett ignored Ava's obnoxious behavior. "Alex, can you please set the table for dinner?" she asked.

Ava jumped up from the couch, and the ice pack slid off her ankle onto the floor. "It's my turn to set the table! I'm doing that!"

"Ava, you need to take it easy," her mom insisted. "Lie down and get that ice pack back on your ankle, please."

Scowling, Ava limped back to the couch, picking up the ice pack along the way. As she propped her leg back up, her dad came home.

Moxy rushed over to greet him. Coach put

his briefcase down in the hallway and came into the living room.

"I heard that ankle of yours was sprained pretty badly," Coach said. "That's tough, Ave."

"Yeah, I know," Ava said.

"Then you know you need to take it easy, right?" Coach asked. "That's the only way you'll heal properly. I've seen it too many times. Kids who get back in the game too fast after an injury, and they end up with a problem the rest of their lives. But you're smarter than that, right?"

Ava sighed. Somehow, Coach could always get through to her when nobody else could.

"Yes, I'm smarter than that," she replied. "I'm a regular genius!"

Coach laughed. "That's my Ava," he said.

"Don't worry, Coach," she said. "I'll take it easy. I won't even run late to my English class like I always do. I'll walk late instead!"

Mrs. Sackett popped her head into the room. "English class?"

"Well, Dr. Rodriguez said I couldn't play basketball, but he didn't say I couldn't go to school," Ava pointed out. "And it would be really bad for me to miss school, wouldn't it?"

Coach and Mrs. Sackett exchanged glances.

"Please promise me that you won't be running through the halls," Mrs. Sackett said.

"Promise!" Ava assured her.

The next morning Ava heard a knock on her door as she was pulling on a T-shirt.

"It's me!" Alex said.

"Come on in," Ava called out, and Alex stepped inside.

"I thought you might need some help making that brace look more . . . fashionable," Alex said, looking down at the bulky black straps around Ava's ankle. "Were you really going to wear shorts to school? In January?"

Ava shrugged. "I can't get my jeans over it," she said, and then she caught the look in her sister's eye. "And no, I am not wearing a skirt!"

Alex wore skirts to school all the time. Today she had on a cute blue skirt that came to just above her knees, paired with a short-sleeved white cropped cardigan over a blue tank top. White knit tights and blue flats completed the outfit.

"But I have the most adorable floral maxi-skirt you could borrow," said Alex. "It would totally cover up that brace."

Ava tried to picture herself in a flowing, flowery skirt. "Um, no thanks. Any other ideas?"

Alex bit her lower lip. "I know!" she blurted out, after a moment. "Wait right here."

She ran out of the room and came back with black leggings and a long red tunic. "This is perfect!" she said. "The black leggings are stretchy enough to go over your brace, and they're black so nobody will notice. And the tunic just looks supercute with the leggings."

Ava nodded. "This is definitely better than a flowery skirt. Thanks."

Alex left, and Ava quickly changed. The leggings did kind of blend in with the brace, she thought. The last thing she wanted was everybody making a big deal about her ankle. Especially the other girls on the basketball team.

But it was no use—everyone still noticed her injury. Ava and Alex got only a few feet down the school hallway when Lindsey spotted them.

"Hi, Alex, hi—Ava, what's wrong with your ankle?"

She said it so loudly that a group of kids

began to gather. Callie and Madison pushed their way through to talk to Ava.

"Is it true? Did you hurt your ankle at the game?" Callie asked.

Ava nodded. "Yeah. I'm sorry. I just came down on it the wrong way."

"You don't have to be sorry!" said Madison sweetly. "We're sorry that you're hurt."

"So, how long will you be out?" Callie asked bluntly.

Ava hated to say it out loud. "Three weeks."

Callie and Madison looked at each other. "Does Coach Rader know?" Callie asked.

Ava didn't know. She knew that her mom had e-mailed him about her doctor's appointment, but did he know about the three weeks?

"I'm not sure," Ava replied. "I'll tell him when I see him sixth period, I guess."

But the moment came sooner than that—she ran into Coach Rader in the hallway as she walked carefully to Spanish class. His eyebrows rose when he saw the brace.

"So what's the verdict?" he asked.

"I can't play for three weeks," Ava replied. "After that, I can play but I have to keep the brace on."

Coach Rader nodded. "We'll miss you out there, Ava."

"I can still come to practices," Ava offered. "You know, so I can learn strategies and stuff."

"Why don't you take it easy this week?" Coach Rader suggested. "Then we can check in on Monday and see how you feel."

Ava sighed. "Yes, Coach," she said, and walked away toward her Spanish classroom.

Take it easy. That was all everybody kept saying. But nobody seemed to understand—how could she take it easy when all she wanted to do was get back on the basketball court?

CHAPTER FIVE

"Hey, is your sister okay?"

Alex looked away from her locker after second period to see Corey standing there, with a worried look in his blue eyes.

"I think not playing basketball hurts more than her ankle does," Alex replied as she shut her locker door.

Corey nodded. "I can't imagine being benched from football right at the start of the season. That would be awful."

Alex walked in the direction of her social studies classroom, and Corey kept in step with her.

"So, um . . . that's a nice sweater," he said, a little awkwardly.

Alex looked down at her white cardigan. "Oh, thanks! It's not as exciting as my ugly sweater, though. That was really something." Thanks to Uncle Scott, her ugly sweater had snowflakes with white twinkling lights.

At the reference to the party, Corey's eyes locked with hers, and they both blushed. Alex knew they were both thinking of the same thing. Their almost-kiss under the falling snow . . .

"Um, hey, Alex."

Max was standing there, wearing a white T-shirt with a green stain right in the center. "I asked Mrs. Bridges yesterday, and she said you're my partner for the social studies project!" he blurted out.

"Oh yeah, that's . . . that's great," Alex said. She looked back at Corey, but the moment was gone—and Corey was already making a hasty retreat.

"See you later!" he called out as he raced off down the hall.

"Yeah, so we'll be working collaboratively," Max said.

"Heard you the first time!" Alex said cheerfully, forcing a smile. She didn't want to be annoyed with Max, but she had been looking forward to being Emily's partner. Not to mention that he had interrupted her moment with Corey. She and Corey hadn't talked much since the party. What might he have said if Max hadn't shown up?

She and Max walked into the classroom, and Alex slid into her seat. When the bell rang, Mrs. Bridges walked out from behind her desk, holding a sheet of paper.

"Okay, I'm going to officially assign your partners for the project," she announced. "And I don't want to hear any complaints about who you're paired with. Here's what's going to happen. Once you're paired up, I want you to sit together. I'm going to be giving you class time to work on the project."

She looked down at the list. "Okay, Alex and Max."

"Poor Alex," Lindsey said. "She's got Sleeping Beauty as a partner!"

Some of the kids laughed, and Alex smiled weakly. She knew Lindsey was trying to be sympathetic to her, but it still felt mean.

"Please keep the commentary to yourself, Lindsey," Mrs. Bridges said. "Okay, Ryan and Shane . . ."

Max picked up his books and moved to an empty seat next to Alex. She quickly opened her social studies folder and got down to business.

"So, I printed out the project rubric from the school website last night," Alex said. She produced two sheets of paper. "Do you need one?"

"Yeah, thanks," Max said gratefully. He looked at it. "So, first we need to choose one of the rights in the Bill of Rights. That's pretty cool. I kind of like the First Amendment. Not abridging free speech and stuff."

He yawned, and seeing him do so made Alex yawn too. She hated when that happened. She had read somewhere that even if you read the word "yawn" on a page, it could make you yawn.

"The First Amendment is a good one, but I think everyone's going to pick that," Alex said. "Maybe we could pick something juicier, like the Fifth Amendment. It means you can't be on trial twice for the same crime."

"Double jeopardy," Max said. "That could be interesting." He yawned again.

Alex felt another copycat yawn coming on, and she covered her mouth.

"Max, what's with all the yawning?" she asked him point-blank.

"Oh, sorry," Max said, but he didn't offer any explanation. And then he yawned again.

Alex laughed. "Not fair!"

By the end of class they had worked out a plan to research their project, and Alex felt like she knew Max a little better. He seemed friendly, and even smart—just really tired.

As she left class, Mrs. Bridges pulled her aside. "Alex, I wanted to talk to you about Max," she said when she rest of the students had left.

"Oh?" Alex asked.

"I purposely put you two together for this project," the teacher said. "I think he could use a little extra help these days, and I would appreciate it if you could give him a hand. You're such a good student, Alex, and you'll be a wonderful role model for him."

Alex smiled. Mrs. Bridges had said exactly the right thing to appeal to Alex—she immediately resolved to help Max as much as she could.

"Of course I'll help him," Alex said.

"Thank you, Alex," Mrs. Bridges said. "I knew I could count on you."

Mrs. Bridges's praise stuck with Alex for the rest of the day. When the last bell rang, she and Ava met by their lockers.

"Mom's finishing up early to give me a ride home," Ava said bitterly, as if that were a punishment of some kind. "Are you coming home now or are you staying after for something?"

Alex shook her head. "I have a meeting for the Variety Show."

Ava raised her eyebrows. "You're involved in that, too? Is there anything you don't do?"

"I'm not performing," Alex said quickly. "Just organizing things."

"Of course you are," said Ava with a grin. "And I'll be comfortably sitting in the audience while you're running around backstage." Then she sighed. "I better go out there before Mom starts to worry," she said, throwing a morose look in the direction of the gym as she limped away.

Alex shook her head. She hated to see her twin so down. She tried to imagine what she would do if she sprained her ankle and were told to take it easy, and her whole body shuddered.

Ava walked outside to find her mother's red SUV parked in a premium spot right by the entrance to the school.

"You must have been waiting here for an hour to snag this spot," Ava said.

"I didn't want you to have to walk too far," Mrs. Sackett said.

"Mom, I've been walking around school all day, and my ankle doesn't even hurt," Ava said, but she winced as she climbed into the passenger seat. "Well, maybe a little."

Mrs. Sackett smiled sympathetically. "You are one tough cookie, Ave."

Ava looked out the window as they drove home. Even though her friends kept complaining that it was chilly, the sun was shining and the leaves on the trees were green. She still had a hard time believing that it was winter. Winter was supposed to be gray and white, not green and blue.

Mrs. Sackett turned the corner, and the car headed toward the park a few blocks away from the Sackett house. Inside the park, a dark-haired boy was shooting hoops by himself.

Ava rolled down the window and waved.

"Hey, Jack!" she called out.

Jack Valdeavano waved back, and Ava felt a pang. Jack was one of the first friends she had made in Ashland, and she had to admit she had a bit of a crush on him as well. On any other sunny day she'd be right there in the park with him, playing basketball. She looked down at her brace and sighed. It was so unfair!

Then her phone chimed, and she looked down to see a text from Kylie.

> You looked so 🙁 all day! Mom says you can come out to the ranch on Saturday to hang. Can you?

Ava read the text out loud so her mom could hear. "So, can I?"

Mrs. Sackett nodded. "Yes, as long as you promise that you won't even think of getting on a horse!"

Another thing I can't do, Ava thought. But she was grateful her mom hadn't said she had to stay home and take it easy!

"Thanks, Mom," Ava said, and she smiled for the first time since she'd sprained her ankle. At least now she had something to look forward to.

CHAPTER SIX

"You know, we don't have to stay inside the house all day," Ava told Kylie, as they ate lunch on Saturday afternoon. "I'm allowed to walk around and stuff."

Kylie smiled. "Yeah, I know. But your mom texted my mom to make sure you weren't going to ride any horses, so I thought it would be depressing if we went out to the stables."

Ava swallowed a bite of her ham sandwich. "Well, it wouldn't hurt to go *look* at the horses, would it?"

Kylie's mom walked into the kitchen. She had the same friendly smile as Kylie, and she wore her hair in braids too, although hers were always tied up in a neat bun.

"Mom, can we go down to the stables if we promise that Ava won't ride?" Kylie asked.

Mrs. McClaire looked at the girls with narrowed eyes. "Do I have your word?"

"Yes!" Ava and Kylie said at the same time.

Kylie's mom smiled. "Then of course. Just clean up after your lunch first, please."

Ava and Kylie grinned at each other and quickly finished their sandwiches and carrot sticks. They cleaned up and headed out to the stables.

"You haven't seen Checkers yet!" Kylie said, practically bouncing with excitement.

"Is Checkers a new horse?" Ava asked.

Kylie nodded. "She's a painted pony, white and black. Gorgeous. She's broken in, but she still needs a lot of training. Mom and Dad are letting me do it," she said proudly.

"She sounds beautiful," Ava said, and when they reached the stables, Ava saw how beautiful the horse really was. Checkers had a black-and-white pattern all over her coat, from her legs up to her mane. She wasn't as tall as some of the other horses at the ranch, but Ava's head still only came up to her shoulder.

Kylie slowly approached her and stroked her nose.

"How's my girl?" she asked, and the horse nodded her head, nuzzling into Kylie's hand.

"It's so cool that you get to train her," Ava remarked.

Kylie nodded. "I should really give her some exercise today. . . ." Her voice trailed off.

"Kylie, you can totally ride her!" Ava said. "Don't worry about me."

"But that's not fair, if I get to ride and you don't," Kylie said.

"It's okay, really!" Ava said, and she meant it. "It'll be fun to see you ride her. Besides, I've got enough pain in my legs right now without being sore from riding, too," she joked.

Kylie looked hesitant, but Ava urged her on.

"Come on, saddle her up!"

"Let me grab my helmet first," Kylie said, grinning.

She left the stable and came back a minute later wearing her riding helmet. Then she attached a rope to Checkers's halter, slowly leading her into the tack room in the stables. The horse calmly followed her. Kylie threw the rope around a ring in the tack room wall and began to saddle her up. She gave Ava a mini lesson as she worked.

"First you put the bit into her mouth," Kylie explained. "That's the hardest part for me. She doesn't seem to like it. But once it fits into that groove into her mouth, she calms down."

Kylie slowly and carefully put on the rest of the tack, explaining each step to Ava as she did it. She pulled the bridle up over Checkers's ears, put a blanket on her back, and then strapped on the saddle and cinched the girth underneath her chest. Finally she attached the straps on the front of the saddle to the horse's breast collar.

With each step, Kylie petted the horse and spoke to her in a soothing voice. "There you go, Checkers. That's my girl," she said.

Ava was impressed. "You are really like a horse whisperer or something."

Kylie looked pleased. "It's in my blood, I guess."

She grabbed the reins, and Ava followed her as they moved to the paddock.

"I've got to ride her inside the fence while she's training," Kylie explained. "I'll just take her around the perimeter a few times."

"I'll take pictures!" Ava offered, holding up her phone.

Kylie brought Checkers inside the paddock and locked the gate behind her. Then she used a set of small steps to climb up on the horse's left side. Checkers skittered a bit as Kylie mounted her, but she calmed down as soon as Kylie had her feet in the stirrups and both hands on the reins.

"Let's go, Checkers!" Kylie said, and the horse broke into a gentle trot. Ava watched her friend go, remembering how nervous she had been the first time Kylie had brought her to the ranch. Watching Kylie ride so confidently made her itch to give it another try.

Then a noise made Ava turn her head.

Vroom! A motorcycle was coming down the long drive to the ranch. In the paddock, Kylie patted Checkers's head.

"Nothing to be afraid of," she told the horse.

But Ava could see thick white smoke pouring from the bike's exhaust. The bike sputtered. And then . . .

Boom! It backfired, making a sound like a loud gunshot.

Startled, Checkers reared up high on her back legs.

"Kylie!" Ava screamed.

Kylie's hands gripped the reins tightly as Checkers lost her footing. The horse stumbled and toppled to the ground, taking Kylie with her!

Her heart pounding, Ava ignored the pain in her ankle as she ran back up to the ranch.

"Kylie needs help!"

"But Checkers is okay, right?" Kylie asked weakly.

"Honey, we've told you that already. She's fine," Mrs. McClaire said. She looked up at Ava, Alex, Coach, and Mrs. Sackett, who were gathered around Kylie's hospital bed.

"A broken leg, and all she can think about is that horse," said Mrs. McClaire.

Mrs. Sackett put an arm on her shoulder. "You look tired, Renée," she said. "How about we go get a cup of coffee and leave the kids alone for a bit?"

Mrs. McClaire looked at her daughter. "Will you be okay? Dad is right outside talking with the nurse."

"I'm not going anywhere, Mom," Kylie joked, and managed a small smile. Mrs. McClaire seemed satisfied.

"All right, but just for a few minutes," she said, and she left the hospital room with Coach and Mrs. Sackett.

It was seven o'clock that night, and Ava had been waiting for hours to see Kylie.

"Kylie, this is all my fault!" she blurted out. "I'm the one who said you should ride Checkers."

"Ava, it's okay," Kylie said. "It was a freak accident."

"We heard you're going to need surgery to fix your broken leg," Alex said.

Kylie nodded. "The doctor says the surgery's nothing major. But I'll be on crutches for a long time. And maybe even in a wheelchair at first."

Then she managed a small smile. "Look at us! We're injury buddies!"

Ava looked down at her small brace and then at Kylie's leg, which was propped up on the bed and supported by a wicked-looking brace with metal rods. Kylie looked small and scared and hurt in the big hospital bed. Suddenly Ava's sprained ankle didn't seem like the end of the world anymore.

"Yeah, but you get some time off school for your injury," Ava said.

"I could bring you all your homework while

you're recovering," Alex offered cheerfully, but Kylie groaned.

"Please! Getting out of homework might be the only good thing that comes out of this!" she said.

"Yeah, what were you thinking, Al?" Ava joked.

Alex's phone chimed before she could answer. She tapped on the screen to see a video from Lindsey. It was the Dancing Divas— the name Lindsey, Rosa, Emily, Charlotte, and Annelise had chosen for their Variety Show act—practicing their dance routine, along with a message.

Dance with us! Practice Tuesday.

Alex rolled her eyes.

"What's up?" Ava asked.

"It's Lindsey," Alex answered. "She and some of my other friends are doing this silly dance routine for the Variety Show, and she keeps asking me to join them. But there is no way I would be caught onstage doing that dance! We all know I'd make a fool of myself. And they keep bugging me to join them, even though I keep saying no."

"Oh no, the Variety Show," Kylie said, and her eyes filled with tears. Ava suddenly realized that she'd never seen her best friend cry before. Poor Kylie!

"Were you going to be in it?" she asked sympathetically, but before Kylie could answer, there was a tap on the open hospital door. It was Owen Rooney, a tall boy with dark, curly hair. He was a receiver on the Ashland Tiger Cubs—and Kylie's sort-of boyfriend.

"Your mom said it would be okay if I came in," Owen said.

"Of course," Kylie said, sitting up a little.

Owen walked closer to the bed and pulled a book out of his jacket pocket. Kylie's eyes got wide.

"Is that the newest Andromeda Saga book?" she asked.

Owen nodded. "Yeah, it just came out this week. I thought you might want to read it while you're stuck in here."

"But you should read it first!" Kylie protested.

"I have my own copy," Owen said. "This one's for you. I thought we could read it at the same time and, you know, talk about it."

Owen handed her the book, and Kylie looked

really cheered up. Ava couldn't help thinking about that time back in Massachusetts when bronchitis had kept her out of school for a week. Her sort-of boyfriend, Charlie, had come by every day to talk to her. He brought her goofy presents like a tiny teddy bear and every sports magazine he could find.

Charlie had a new girlfriend now, and he and Ava didn't text as much anymore—especially now that the Patriots' season was over. *I haven't thought about Charlie in a while,* she realized wistfully.

Alex nudged her out of her reverie. "We should probably, you know, leave these guys alone," she whispered.

Ava looked up and saw that Owen and Kylie were deep in conversation about some alien princess or something and nodded to her sister.

"Kylie, I'll come back and visit," Ava promised. "And I'll make sure Alex *doesn't* bring your homework."

"That was a genuinely nice offer," Alex protested as Ava dragged her out of the room.

They found their parents talking with Mr. and Mrs. McClaire. After a round of good-byes, the Sacketts headed home.

"Thanks for bringing me," Ava said on the ride home.

"Of course, sweetheart!" said Mrs. Sackett. "I'm just glad that Kylie is going to be okay."

"So am I," said Ava.

And I'm going to be okay too, she thought. *From now on, no more moping around!*

CHAPTER SEVEN

"Uncle Scott, I have to catch the bus in twenty minutes!" Alex said, knocking on the bathroom door.

"I just need three more minutes, Alex!" Uncle Scott called through the door. "I've got to finish shaving and then use my Neti pot. I need my sinuses clear for this interview!"

Ava walked past Alex's open door on her way downstairs.

"Neti pot? Is that the thing that looks like a teapot in the downstairs medicine cabinet?" Ava asked.

Alex nodded. "Right. But it's not a teapot. He uses it to clean out his nostrils."

"Seriously? That's gross!" Ava said. "That is almost enough to make me not want to eat breakfast, except that I am so hungry I could eat three breakfasts!" Then she walked off.

Alex sighed and pounded on the bathroom door again. "Why are you in *our* bathroom, exactly?" she asked.

She heard the sound of running water. It stopped, and then her uncle answered.

"Because your dad was in the shower downstairs when I woke up, and I have an early interview," Uncle Scott replied. "Can't you go eat breakfast and then use the bathroom when I'm done?"

Alex frowned. She had her morning routine worked out: She got up and showered before Ava even opened her eyes. Then she got dressed and went back into the bathroom to tame her stray curls with a flat iron. *Then* breakfast.

She glanced at the clock.

"Fine!" she said, and headed downstairs.

"Alex! You sound like an elephant," Coach said as Alex continued stomping into the kitchen.

"It's Uncle Scott," Alex said. "He's disturbing my morning routine."

"Oh boy," said Tommy, digging into a huge

bowl of oatmeal and sliced bananas in front of him. "That's a criminal offense in Alex's book. Poor Uncle Scott."

Mrs. Sackett came in through the back door with Moxy on a leash.

"What about Uncle Scott?" she asked.

"He's disturbing Alex's morning routine," Ava reported.

"Oh, right, the job interview!" Mrs. Sackett said, sounding exceedingly chipper. "Alex, you let your uncle do whatever he needs to do to get ready. Besides, it looks like you're ready for school anyway."

Alex grabbed a banana from the basket on the counter. "For your information, I have not tamed this wayward strand of hair," she said, yanking on it to demonstrate its waywardness. "It constantly gets in my right eye. I won't be able to concentrate in school all day if I don't get back up in that bathroom and use my flat iron on it. Is that what you want?"

Just then Uncle Scott came bounding down the stairs. Alex had to admit that he looked job-interview ready. He was freshly shaven, and he'd styled his wavy brown hair with just the right amount of gel. He wore a crisp blue dress shirt with a red tie and dark blue pants.

"Looking good, bro," Coach said.

"Yes, your nostrils look especially clean," joked Ava.

"Mock all you want, but that Neti pot keeps me healthy," Uncle Scott retorted.

"Good luck!" Alex said as she raced past him and back up the stairs to fix her wayward lock.

She was heating up her flat iron when her phone chimed with a text from Emily.

Home with a cold! ☹

Oh no, feel better!

Alex reached for the flat iron—it wasn't quite hot yet, but she was out of time. Her curl went untamed, and Alex spent the whole day brushing it away from her face. She was still brushing it away as she entered third-period social studies.

Max lifted his head up from his desk as Alex walked past. "What's up?" he asked. "You look somewhat perturbed."

That's an odd way of putting it, Alex thought, *but very observant.*

"Oh, it's just . . . families can be challenging, you know?" she asked, thinking of Uncle Scott.

Max nodded. "Tell me about it," he said, and then he started to put his head back down on his desk again.

"Wait!" Alex said. "We need to meet in the library to do our research for the project. Are you free tomorrow after school?"

"What?" Max looked confused for a minute. "Oh yeah, sure."

Lindsey walked past Alex and gave her a look that clearly meant, *What are you talking to him for?* Alex was almost going to say something when Mrs. Bridges walked in and the bell rang.

"All right, everyone open up to page one hundred twenty," she announced, and Alex forgot about Lindsey's look as the lesson began.

But as soon as the last bell rang, Lindsey charged up to Alex's desk. Rosa hung behind her, curious.

"Alex, I heard you talking to Max. Why are you making plans with him when he'll probably sleep through your study session anyway? Tomorrow is dance practice. I thought you were too busy to dance with us," she said accusingly.

Alex quickly glanced in Max's direction. He had just gotten up from his desk, and Alex was sure he had heard Lindsey. She cringed.

"Lindsey, I keep telling you, it's not just that I'm too busy, it's also that I can't dance," Alex said, trying to be polite.

"That's just an excuse," Lindsey said. "Besides, dancing with us is better than working on some lame report with a loser!"

She emphasized the last word, looking at Max as he made his way out the door behind Mrs. Bridges.

That was too much for Alex. She couldn't keep ignoring Lindsey's nasty remarks about Max. Not anymore.

"Listen, Lindsey, Max is not a loser," Alex said.

Lindsey laughed. "Are you serious? He never changes his clothes or even showers, for that matter. He falls asleep all the time. That is super lame!"

"Oh yeah?" Alex shot back, getting angrier and angrier. Why was her friend being so mean? "Well . . . well, maybe I don't want to be in your dance because I think your whole routine is lame!"

Lindsey's jaw dropped, and behind her, Rosa gasped.

"If that's how you feel," Lindsey said, her voice cold as ice. "Come on, Rosa."

Alex stood, frozen, as Lindsey and Rosa walked away.

That was not *the right way to handle things,* she scolded herself. She had worked so hard to become friends with Lindsey, and now everything was ruined!

Well, Lindsey ruined it too, by being so mean to Max, a little voice inside her reminded Alex. But it didn't help. Because Alex knew that by insulting the dance routine, she had not only insulted Lindsey, but Rosa, Annelise, Charlotte—and Emily.

"Oh no," Alex groaned. Once Lindsey told everyone what she had said, she wouldn't have a friend left in Ashland!

CHAPTER EIGHT

"Two cheeseburgers, extra ketchup," Ava announced, holding up a greasy white paper bag as she walked into Kylie's hospital room later that afternoon.

"Ava, you're the best," Kylie said, sitting up in her hospital bed. Ava pulled a green plastic chair closer to Kylie's bed and sat down. She thought her friend still looked really tired. Her braids were pulled back behind her neck.

"When you texted me that you had creamed chicken with peas for dinner on Sunday, I thought you might appreciate these," Ava said, handing Kylie the bag. "Mom stopped at Burger Hut on the way here."

"Tell her thanks," Kylie said, biting into the burger. "Oh wow, that's good."

"How does your leg feel after the surgery?" Ava asked.

"It hurts pretty badly, but the medicine helps," Kylie said. "I just want to get out of here! I'm going crazy. But the doctor says I might have to say another couple of days." She sighed.

"Well, you didn't miss much at school," Ava reported, trying to remember if anything interesting had happened. "Oh yeah. During lunch, Billy Scarbek balanced a chair on his nose. He said he was practicing for the Variety Show."

Kylie stopped chewing and looked down at her hands.

"Hey, you looked sad when Alex mentioned the Variety Show on Saturday, too," Ava said, remembering. "You weren't going to be in it, were you?"

Kylie put down the cheeseburger she was eating and took a deep breath. "Ava, I need to tell you something about me that you don't know," she said solemnly.

"Okay, now I'm in suspense. What is it?" Ava asked.

"I love line dancing," Kylie blurted out. "I know

you probably think it's goofy, being from the East Coast and everything, but it's actually a lot of fun. I learned when I was a little kid."

"Well, you are wrong about me thinking line dancing is silly, because I don't even know what line dancing is," Ava admitted.

Kylie picked up her phone and found a video clip. Then she handed it to Ava.

"This is line dancing. You've probably seen it in movies and stuff."

Ava looked at the video playing on the phone. Three rows of people wearing cowboy hats were dancing in perfect step. They clapped and slapped their knees in time with the music. Ava thought the tune was pretty catchy.

"Hey, this is cool," Ava said. "It's pretty amazing the way everybody does the steps at exactly the same time, and they keep the lines straight too."

Kylie smiled. "I'm glad you don't think it's dumb. Anyway, since the theme this year is Wild West, my line-dancing friends and I were really excited to have an act in the Variety Show. When I texted them that I broke my leg, I could tell they were upset. The dance works with five people, but it looks a lot better with six."

Kylie looked really sad, and Ava felt so bad

for her friend. She wanted to do anything she could to make Kylie feel better. Before she could really think about it, she blurted out, "I'll take your place!"

Kylie looked surprised. "Ava, that's sweet, but what about your ankle?"

"It's been a week already, and it doesn't even hurt," Ava countered. "I'm allowed to walk on the brace, I just can't jump and run and stuff. It doesn't look like there's any of that in the video."

Kylie looked thoughtful. "No, there isn't, really. I mean, you'd probably be okay . . . but you didn't even know what line dancing was until I told you!"

"I know, but it doesn't look that hard," Ava said. "I mean, I'm sure you need to practice a lot, but I learned a lot of complicated cheer-leading routines when I was pretending to be Alex, right?"

Kylie shook her head. "Yeah, and that worked out really great," she said sarcastically.

Ava laughed. At the beginning of the school year, Alex wanted to impress her friends by trying out for cheerleading, but she knew how terrible she would be at it. So Ava had agreed to dress like Alex and try out in her place. She was supposed to do well enough to be respectable, but not well enough to make the team. But she had really gotten into it, and Alex (actually Ava) had made the team! Then, when the real Alex took her place on the team, it had been a disaster.

"Okay, that wasn't the smartest thing I've ever done," Ava admitted. "But the point is that I was really great at cheerleading. And on the football field, I have to follow complicated plays all the time. So I should be able to figure out line dancing, right?"

Kylie looked amused. "You know, it just might work," she said. "Okay, do you know Carly Hermano?"

"Yeah, she's a cheerleader," Ava replied. "And I think she's on student council with Alex."

Kylie nodded. "So, Carly and I were in dance class together when we were little. She's the one who's leading the dance. I'll text her and let her know you're going to replace me."

She had a funny grin on her face when she said it.

"You don't think I can do it, do you?" Ava asked. Kylie's skepticism made her even more determined to help the line dance be the best act at the Variety Show.

"I think that it's really nice of you to do it, and I think it's going to be really fun to watch," Kylie replied. "I just hope I'll get out of this hospital before the big night!"

"Of course you will," Ava assured her.

Then she realized that she had just committed to performing a traditional Texas dance in front of a crowd filled with native Texans, and she had just moved to Texas and had never even heard of line dancing before.

What have I gotten myself into? she wondered.

CHAPTER NINE

"Why do you keep checking your phone?" Ava asked her sister on the bus ride to school the next morning.

Alex looked around to see who was sitting near them, and then spoke in a low voice.

"It's a long story, but I kind of insulted the dance routine that all my friends are doing for the Variety Show," she explained. "I texted Emily last night asking if I could talk to her, but I think Lindsey must have gotten to her first, because Emily hasn't texted me back. I don't know if it's because she's mad at me or because she's still feeling bad from her cold."

"What do you mean, 'kind of' insulted?" Ava asked.

Alex sighed. "I told Lindsey it was lame. But she was being mean, and I couldn't help myself."

"Well, I'm sure Emily will understand," Ava told her. "She's nice. She knows how Lindsey can be sometimes."

"I hope so," Alex said anxiously.

"Anyway, I didn't tell you my news," Ava said. "I'm going to be in the Variety Show. I'm taking Kylie's place in a line dancing thing."

Alex's eyes got wide. "You mean Toe the Line?"

"Toe the Line?" Ava repeated.

"Yeah, it's the name of the line dancing group," Alex explained. "It's a pun. You know, T-O-E . . ."

"Yeah, I get it," Ava said. "Kylie didn't say they had a name."

"Well, everyone on the committee is super excited about it," Alex reported. "Apparently, they're amazing and they brought the house down last year." She looked at Ava. "Line dancing can be pretty complicated. Are you sure you're up for this? I mean, with your sprained ankle and all."

"I'm up for it," Ava said firmly.

Alex studied her sister's face. She could see the nervousness behind her confident statement. But she knew that once Ava was determined to do something, there was no talking her out of it. She had fought hard to become the only girl on the boys' football team. And she had never given up when their parents refused to let her play basketball. Besides, she really had been amazing during cheerleading tryouts.

"I'm sure you'll be great," Alex said supportively.

The school bus made a noise like a groaning dinosaur and pulled up in front of school. When Alex got off the bus, she spotted Emily's blond head among the crowd of students walking into school.

"See you later," Alex told Ava, jogging toward her friend.

"Emily!" she called out.

Emily turned. She didn't smile when she saw Alex, but she didn't look upset, either. She marched right toward her.

"Do you really think our dance routine is lame?" Emily asked directly.

"That's what I wanted to explain," Alex said. "Why I texted you last night. But you didn't text back."

Emily sighed. "Lindsey was texting me like crazy too, and I didn't want to get into some text war. So why don't you explain, then?"

The girls walked into the school and leaned against a wall in the front hallway.

"I'm so sorry," Alex said. "We were in social studies class, and Lindsey was saying mean things about Max. She's been saying mean things about him for days now. I think she's still mad at him for embarrassing her."

"Yeah, I know," Emily admitted. "I've been wanting to say something to her about it, but . . . what does that have to do with our dance routine, anyway? That's the part I don't get."

"Well, she said it was lame that I was working on my project with Max instead of joining your dance act, and that Max was lame, so I just said that the dance routine was lame," Alex said. "I didn't mean it. Lindsey just pushed me too far."

Emily nodded. "Rosa said it happened something like that. I understand."

"So does that mean we're good?" Alex asked. "Because I really, really, really am sorry."

Emily smiled. "Yeah, we're good."

Alex smiled back, relieved—until she remembered that just because Emily forgave her didn't mean Lindsey would. "I know you're good, but what about everybody else?"

"I think Rosa understands," Emily replied. "Annelise and Charlotte will too, once I explain it to them. But Lindsey is really fuming about it."

Alex nodded. "I'll make it right with Lindsey, I promise."

The first morning bell rang, and the girls scurried to their lockers. Alex felt comforted knowing that Emily understood and was still her friend, but she knew that making things right with Lindsey wouldn't be easy. She and Lindsey had gotten off on the wrong foot right from the start, and it had taken months for them to finally become friends. This might be the last straw in their friendship.

Alex's hunches were right. In social studies, Lindsey made a point never to look in Alex's direction. And when Max approached Alex and said he would meet her in the library after school, Lindsey whispered something to Rosa and then laughed really loudly.

At lunch Lindsey made it very obvious that she was talking only to Annelise, Charlotte, Rosa, and Emily. She acted like Alex was invisible at the table. Alex knew that talking with her then wouldn't have done any good, so she spent most of the lunch hour listening to a conversation Ava and Jack were having about college basketball and tried to act like everything was normal. She started to wonder if apologizing to Lindsey was even worth it. She could be such a difficult person!

Do I really need a friend like that? Alex wondered. But the problem was that Lindsey was friends with Emily, and everyone else Alex liked. She had to get along with Lindsey, or things would be forever awkward anytime she hung out with her friends. And Lindsey was usually a nice person, and a lot of fun to be around—Alex didn't know why she was still holding a grudge against Max.

But when and how she would make it right to Lindsey—that was what she had to figure out. She had other things to do in the meantime.

Like working with Max on their social studies project, for one. When the final bell rang, she first headed to the auditorium to see Chloe Klein, the sixth-grade class president. Chloe was one of the other student council members working behind the scenes on the Variety Show. Alex found her backstage, writing in a notebook.

"So, we've got some acts rehearsing today," Chloe informed her. "I'm going to talk with them to find out what kind of lighting they need and what kind of props they're using."

"Sorry I can't help today," Alex said.

"That's okay. Kendall and Jerome will be here soon," Chloe said. "You can be here on Thursday, right? We're going to start choosing the lineup and talking about the program."

"No problem," said Alex. "See you then."

As she walked out of the auditorium, she saw a boy twirling a lasso and singing onstage. Emily, Lindsey, Rosa, Charlotte, and Annelise sat in the seats, waiting their turn. Emily waved at Alex, but Lindsey turned her head just as Alex walked by.

Alex sighed and hurried to the school library. Max was sitting at a table with his social studies book open and his head resting on it, like a pillow.

"Max!" Alex hissed in a loud whisper as she sat down.

Max jolted awake. "What? Oh, hey, Alex."

Alex took her social studies folder out of her backpack and opened it up.

"So, I made an outline of the project," Alex

began, taking out a sheet of paper to show him. "I thought maybe we could divide up the research."

Max picked up the paper and read out loud. "Research the history of the Fifth Amendment. Research three important Fifth Amendment cases. Describe why the Fifth Amendment is important to students. List reasons." He groaned and put down his head again. "This is so much!"

"It won't be so bad if we divide it up," Alex said encouragingly. "And there are two of us working on it, so we can each take a part of the project we're interested in. Are you more interested in the history of how the amendment was created, or the court cases?"

Max seemed to brighten a little. "The court cases, I guess. I started looking stuff up last night, and there were some pretty serious cases where people were pressured into confessing crimes when the Fifth Amendment could have helped them."

"Okay, so why don't you start with one court case, and I'll start with the history of the amendment, and then we'll check in with each other in a couple of days," Alex suggested.

Max frowned. "I guess. It'll be pretty hard for

me to work on it at home. I'll have to do everything here, but the library doesn't stay open that late."

"There's always the town library," Alex reminded him. She was curious about why he couldn't do homework at home but didn't want to ask. That felt like prying.

"I know, but it's on the other side of town from where I live, and I can't get a ride," Max said.

"So, we might as well get started now," Alex said, determined to keep Max from being negative about every suggestion she made. "Why don't you start by looking online and seeing what books the library has on the subject? We need at least two books in our bibliography."

"Sure," Max said, and he slid out of his seat and made his way over to the library computer station.

Alex looked down at her outline, but she was distracted thinking about Lindsey. She had to stop this before it got any worse. Maybe she could talk to Lindsey before the Dancing Divas started their practice.

Alex left her folder on the table, let Max know she'd be right back, and went back to the auditorium. She found Lindsey and the others still waiting in their seats.

Alex slid into the row behind them. The girls got quiet, and Lindsey once again turned her head.

"Lindsey, can we talk, please?" Alex asked. "I need to apologize to you."

Lindsey's head spun around. "Yes?" she asked.

"I really didn't mean to say your act was lame, honestly," Alex said. "I just got upset when you called Max lame, and a loser, and—"

"There you go, defending Max," Lindsey said. "You didn't defend *me* when he made fun of me."

"But I don't think he *was* making fun of you," Alex said. "And anyway, the bell rang right after, and—"

"And you'd rather hang out with Max than be in our *lame* dance group," Lindsey interrupted.

"Lindsey, I am so sorry I said that! Honestly!" Alex insisted.

"Apology *not* accepted," Lindsey said, and she turned away from Alex again.

Alex looked at Emily for some guidance, but Emily just shook her head. It was no use. Not now, anyway.

"Well, if you're ever ready to accept my apology, just come find me," Alex said to the back of

Lindsey's head, maybe a little too sharply, and then she walked off.

That was frustrating, she thought. But at least she felt that she understood Lindsey a little bit more. Lindsey went to great lengths not to be embarrassed. She hadn't wanted Alex to know she got the free school lunch or that she bought her clothes in the thrift shop. Max's "preignition" comment must have gotten to her more than Alex realized—and it hadn't helped that Alex had smiled at it. And now she and Max were project partners. Lindsey probably thought Alex was a traitor. How was she supposed to fix that?

Back in the library, Max was sitting at the table. When Alex approached, he quickly opened a book titled *The History of the Bill of Rights* and started leafing through it, as though he wanted Alex to think he'd been reading it the whole time.

That struck Alex as odd, but then again, Max was a little odd anyway. She sat down and noticed some pages sticking out of her social studies folder. *Did I leave them like that?* she briefly wondered, but then quickly forgot about it.

"So, this book looks pretty good," Max said. "But maybe it's something you can use. I'm not finding any court cases in here."

"Thanks," Alex said, taking the book from him. "Maybe we can do some online research for that."

The two of them worked in the library until it closed, and then they walked out to the front of the school together. Alex saw Tommy waiting for her right in front of the school. She walked toward the car, their dad's sedan, and then stopped.

"Max, do you have a ride?" she asked.

"Um, my stepmom's supposed to pick me up," Max said, looking at his phone. "I tried texting her, but she's not answering."

"Where do you live?" Alex asked.

"In Magnolia Terrace," Max replied.

"I know where that neighborhood is. Tommy will give you a ride home," Alex said, and motioned for Max to follow her.

He flashed her a grateful look as they approached Tommy's car.

"Can you please give Max a ride?" Alex asked her brother. "He lives in Magnolia Terrace."

"Sure, hop in," Tommy said.

Alex sat shotgun, and Max climbed into the back. It took only a few minutes to get to Max's home, a white ranch house in a quiet neighborhood. Alex couldn't help noticing that the grass was a little long in the front yard.

"Okay, thanks," Max said, and darted inside.

"Who was that?" Tommy asked as he pulled out of the driveway.

"My social studies project partner," Alex explained. "He's nice but a little strange, and I wonder if something else is going on. I can't quite figure him out."

Tommy laughed. "If I know you, Alex, you won't stop until you do!"

CHAPTER TEN

Ava spent the hour after school sitting on the bleachers in the gym, watching her basketball team practice. Everyone cheered when she came in, and it was more fun than she thought it would be to watch them run drills. She paid close attention to everything Coach Rader said—when it came time for her to get back in the game, she wanted to be ready.

Then her phone beeped at four o'clock, reminding her she had somewhere to be. She waved good-bye to her team and headed for the auditorium.

Carly Hermano had approached her at lunch-time, all smiles.

"Kylie said you would take her place in the line dance," Carly said. "That is awesome!"

"I feel so bad for Kylie," Ava said, "and if it helps you guys to have a sixth person, I'll do it. I'm excited to learn how to line dance."

Carly's smile faded a bit. "You mean you've never done it?"

"Um, no, didn't Kylie tell you?" Ava asked, starting to feel nervous.

"No, but I'm sure you'll work out just fine," Carly replied.

"I'm good on my feet, honestly," Ava said, and Carly's gaze drifted down to her ankle. "Well, except for that. But that was an accident."

"Okay. We're practicing in the auditorium at four o'clock. I'll call out the steps as we dance, and you can just follow along," Carly said.

Ava nodded. "Yeah, sure. I'll see you then."

So Ava's palms were a little sweaty as she headed to the auditorium. What if the other dancers didn't want her to join them? And what if she couldn't keep up?

The first of her fears disappeared when she entered the auditorium.

"Hey, it's Ava!" Carly called from the stage. "Come on up!"

Four other kids stood onstage with Carly, and Ava vaguely knew them all from seeing them around school.

"Everybody, this is Kylie's friend Ava," said Carly. Then she pointed to a girl who wore her black hair in a high ponytail.

"This is Hana," Carly said, and then she proceeded to introduce Ava to the rest of the group. Keshawn, a tall, skinny boy; Kimberly, a petite blond girl; and David, a short boy with glasses, who pointed his fingers like pistols in the air when Carly said his name and pretended to shoot them.

"Pleased to meet you, pardner," he said. "Welcome to Toe the Line."

"I hope I can help out," Ava said. "I've never line danced before."

"I've seen you on the football field. You're fast on your feet," Keshawn said, and Ava blushed.

"Thanks," she said.

"Okay, let's line up," Carly said, and the dancers fell into two rows. In the front was David, then Carly, then Kimberly. Keshawn stood behind Carly, Hana stood behind Kimberly, and Carly instructed Ava to stand behind David.

At least I'm in the second row, Ava thought. *If*

I mess up, it won't be too noticeable, right?

Carly turned to look at the back row. "Okay, I'm going to call out the steps as we go," she said. "Ava, just try to copy what we're doing, okay?"

"Okay!" Ava said.

Carly called offstage. "All right, Chloe!"

Chloe pressed a button on the sound system, and the opening strains of a country-and-western song filled the air. After a few beats, Carly called out, "Walk forward!"

That sounded easy enough to Ava. She took a step forward, watching Keshawn next to her. He took a step forward, lifted up his left foot, and clapped. Ava tried to copy him, but her clap came one beat after everyone else's.

"Grapevine right!" Carly called out.

Grapevine? Ava had no idea what that meant. She took some steps to the right but then noticed that the others were moving sideways, crossing one foot behind the other as they moved. By the time she mimicked the move, Carly was already calling out the next one.

"Grapevine left!"

Ava took another sideways step left and tried to move her right leg behind her left leg, but she was a little slower than the others. When she finally made the move, Keshawn was already moving back toward her, and they bumped into each other.

"Sorry!" Ava said, and Keshawn just smiled at her.

"Step, tap! Step, tap!" Carly was saying, and Ava had to look down at Keshawn's feet to see what that meant. By the time Carly called out the next move, something about a jazz box, Ava had decided that marching in place was the best thing to do.

What have I gotten myself into? she wondered.

"Pivot right!" Carly called out, and everyone made a half turn to the right—except Ava, who turned left in her confusion. As she made the turn, she saw two boys enter the auditorium from the corner of her eye: Jack Valdeavano and Spencer Mills.

Oh no, Ava thought. Jack was going to think she was the worst line dancer in the world—which was true! She prayed that nobody could see her behind David, but since David was a head shorter than she was, she knew that wasn't likely. She tried to concentrate on what Carly was saying.

"Kick left!" Carly called out, and Ava turned and gave an enthusiastic kick—which hit Keshawn right in the back of the knee.

"Sorry!" Ava hissed again, and she could feel her face turning bright red. When the song finally ended, she could feel the relief through her whole body.

Carly clapped her hands.

"Nice effort, everybody!" she said in her best cheerleader voice. Then she looked at Ava. "I guess that brace is giving you some trouble, right?"

"Oh, right, the brace," Ava said, happy to have an excuse. But she knew the truth—she had no idea how to line dance!

"We've all been practicing this for weeks," Keshawn said kindly. "I can write down the steps for you so you can practice them at home."

"That would be amazing," Ava said gratefully.

"I'll send them to your school e-mail," Keshawn offered, just as Chloe came out onstage.

"Okay, clear the stage, please!" Chloe said. "Jack and Spencer, you're up!"

Jack grinned at Ava as they crossed paths. "That was really special up there," he said.

Ava blushed. "It was my first time," she

explained. "I'm just filling in for Kylie."

"I'm sure you'll pick it up," Jack said.

"So, what are you and Spencer doing?" Ava asked. Spencer was a member of the drama club, and Ava hadn't known that he and Jack were friends.

"Hip-hop," Jack replied. Ava raised her eyebrows. "Yeah, he and I took hip-hop dance classes in fifth and sixth grade."

"I have to see this!" Ava said, and she checked the time on her phone. Her mom had said to text her when practice was done. She settled into a front-row seat to watch.

Jack and Spencer shook out their limbs for a few seconds, and then the music began. The two of them started locking, popping, and rolling all over the stage, moving in perfect time with each other.

"Woo-hoo!" Ava cheered. They were awesome!

And then it hit her. This was a serious Variety Show. If she didn't figure out how to line dance, she might never live it down!

CHAPTER ELEVEN

The rest of the week was difficult for Alex. Lindsey still refused to speak to her, making every day at lunch awkward. Luckily, she had the social studies research to keep her busy, as well as the plans for the Variety Show.

On Thursday Alex met with the other members of the Variety Show committee after school. Besides Chloe there was Kendall, the eighth-grade class secretary, and Jerome, Chloe's vice president in the sixth grade.

Chloe opened up a notebook with a marbled cover.

"Okay, we have nineteen acts so far, and people are still signing up," she reported. "We've got twelve singers, six dance acts, and one guy balancing a chair on his nose."

"Wow, that's a lot of musical acts," Alex remarked. "Is that what it's always like?"

"Not usually," Kendall said. "Last year Roman Hitchcock did a comedy routine, but he's in high school now. And two years ago some kid did magic."

"That would be a nice break from all the singing," Alex said. "Do we know anybody who does magic?"

"No, but there's this kid in my math class who's pretty funny," said Jerome. "Maybe he could tell some jokes or something."

"Okay, let's forget the acts for a second. How are we doing on the program?" Kendall asked. "Last year Julie O'Connor did the art for the cover, but she's in high school now too."

"So all the talented kids graduated?" Chloe asked. "Great."

"I'm pretty artistic," Alex said. "I could try to come up with something."

"The cover just has to go with the theme," Kendall said. "Wild West. And it has to say, 'Ashland Middle School Variety Show' and the date."

Alex wrote quickly as Kendall was speaking. "Got it!" she said.

In social studies class the next day, Alex finished her workbook pages early and used the time to sketch out the idea she had for the program cover—a cowboy hat surrounded by a lasso. Drawing the hat was easy, but getting the lasso just right was more difficult than she'd thought it would be. She was erasing some lines on her latest sketch when the bell rang.

"Alex, Max, may I please see you both?" Mrs. Bridges asked.

Alex figured she wanted to check in on their report, or to see how Max was doing with Alex's help. But she wasn't expecting what happened next.

The teacher opened a folder and pulled out two papers—the homework assignment they had turned in on Wednesday. Alex immediately recognized her own handwriting on one paper, and the other one was Max's.

"So when I was grading Wednesday's homework, I noticed something," Mrs. Bridges began. "Your answers are exactly the same—word for word."

Alex got a sinking feeling. How could that have happened?

"Alex, I asked you to help Max, not do his homework for him," Mrs. Bridges said.

Then Alex remembered—how Max had acted strange when she got back to the library on Tuesday, and how her papers were sticking out of her folder. He must have copied off her paper while she was trying to apologize to Lindsey! Mrs. Bridges had given the class the assignment on Monday and Alex had finished it on Monday night. It was in her folder, waiting to be handed in.

She glared at Max and opened her mouth to tell Mrs. Bridges what happened, but stopped when she saw the mortified look on his face. She closed her mouth. She had to tell the truth— or did she?

"Maybe you thought you were helping, but I'm going to have to talk with the principal about consequences," Mrs. Bridges said. "This kind of cheating is taken very seriously, especially now that you're in seventh grade."

Alex held her tongue. Back at her old school in Boston, she remembered when a kid in her class had been caught cheating. He'd been given a warning and told if he did it again, he would be suspended. Alex knew that there was no danger of her ever being accused of cheating again, so the worst that would happen would probably be a warning. Which definitely stung, but she couldn't bear to tell on Max. He just looked so sad and sorry.

"That's all, Alex," Mrs. Bridges said. "Max, I still have some things to say to you."

Alex nodded and walked out the door, but her curiosity got the better of her. She hung back, listening.

"Max, you're going to be on academic probation soon if you don't keep your grades up," she said. "You're a smart kid. You don't need to cheat. You can come to me for help at any time, okay?"

"Okay," Max mumbled. Alex heard him start to leave. She took a few steps down the hall so he wouldn't know she had been listening. She stepped in front of him as he walked past.

"Max, I know what happened," she said. "You copied my homework at the library on Tuesday!"

"I did not!" he insisted, but he was looking down at his sneakers, not at Alex's face.

"Max, I saw that my folder was messed up," she said, starting to feel more angry at him than sorry for him. "How else did you end up with the same answers as I did?"

"Right, like you're so smart that the only way it happened is if I copied from you," Max said. "How do I know that you didn't copy from me?"

"Because I didn't!" Alex replied.

"Whatever," Max said, and he pushed past her.

Alex stared after him, feeling hurt. She didn't have time to dwell on it, though, because she was going to be late to her next class.

What am I doing wrong? she wondered as she hurried through the halls. It didn't seem right. She had ruined her friendship with Lindsey by standing up for Max. She hadn't ratted him out to Mrs. Bridges. And for what? So he could be a jerk to her?

She jammed her books into her locker just as the bell rang.

She would be so happy once this terrible week was over!

CHAPTER TWELVE

Alex did a double take when she passed by the kitchen Saturday morning and saw Ava standing there in her basketball uniform.

"Ava! You're not supposed to be playing yet. It hasn't been three weeks," she said.

"Yes, Dr. Alex, I know," Ava said. "But the game is against Lewisville this morning, and I'm going to stay on the sidelines. I'm still a member of the team, you know."

"I know," said Alex, moving to the refrigerator and pulling out a carton of milk. "But won't it be kind of hard for you, sitting there?"

"Yes, but at least I'll be at the game," Ava replied.

"That's the spirit," Coach said, entering the room. "You ready?"

Ava nodded. "Let's go!"

Ava wasn't prepared for the response as she walked into the gym at Lewisville Middle School.

"Ava!"

Callie and Madison ran toward her, and each of them high-fived her. The other players gathered around, asking questions all at the same time.

"Does it hurt?"

"Can you play today?"

"I can't play for, like, another week," Ava informed them. "Believe me, I'm itching to get back on the court!"

Coach Rader blew his whistle, and the other girls ran off to do warm-ups. Ava took her place on the bench with a little sigh.

No moping! she reminded herself. *Kylie isn't even back in school yet!*

All thoughts of moping left her mind as soon as the game started. She watched every move her teammates made, and she was surprised to realize how much she could learn just by watching. Like how Tessa was a cautious passer, and how Tamara seemed to be getting better and better—and was being sort of a ball hog.

Ava cheered when her team scored, and was literally on the edge of her seat when Madison scored the winning basket in the last thirty seconds of the game. The Cubs got together in a huddle, and Callie pulled in Ava to join them.

"You guys did great," Ava said.

"And we'll do even better when you're playing with us again," Callie responded. Ava beamed.

After the game, Coach brought Ava out to the ranch for a visit with Kylie.

"See? I didn't even need the wheelchair. I can get around just fine on these," Kylie bragged, as she crossed her living room quickly using her crutches.

"You are a speed demon," Ava agreed. "Now, please sit down so I can finally sign your cast!" She waved the marker she held at Kylie.

Kylie propped her leg up on the coffee table. Her parents had already signed it, and Ava saw that Owen had written:

Andromeda United! ♡ Owen

"Ooh, heart Owen," Ava said, wiggling her eyebrows.

"I know, isn't he sweet?" Kylie asked, blushing. "I keep wanting to draw all over this cast, like a cool alien landscape or something, but Mom says I have to leave some space because everyone's going to want to sign it."

"Like me," Ava said, and the marker hovered over the cast as she thought about what to write. Something nice? Something inspirational? Something funny?

Funny won out.

Help! I'm trapped inside this cast! ☺ Ava

Kylie laughed. "Oh my gosh, it really does feel like hundreds of tiny little creatures are trapped in there," she said. "It's already itching like crazy!"

"That stinks," said Ava. "We should do something to take your mind off it. How about a board game?"

Kylie brightened. "Citizens of Elvador?" she asked.

Ava stifled a groan. She had been thinking of something easy, like where you have to draw pictures to guess words. Citizens of Elvador was one of those complicated board games where you created societies and went on quests and searched for gold. Kylie loved to play it with Owen. Ava had never been interested in playing it, but she couldn't say no to Kylie now.

Kylie got back on her crutches. "Going to the game closet! Be right back!"

Two hours later, Ava was absorbed in the game, much to her own surprise.

"Okay, my elves are exploring this mountain cave," she said, moving her piece along the board.

"Are you sure you want to do that?" Kylie asked.

Ava knew Kylie was trying to give her a warning, but she didn't care. She wanted to see what happened. Kylie turned over a card in front of the cave.

"Dragon!" Kylie cried. "Your elves are not strong enough to withstand the attack."

She moved a playing piece over to Ava's citadel. "Now that you are unguarded, I claim your citadel. I win!"

Ava sat back on her chair. "Wow, that was intense."

Then Kylie's phone chimed, and she picked it up. "It's Keshawn, texting to ask if I'm okay," she said. "He's so nice. I think I've been in every class with him since kindergarten."

Then she looked up at Ava. "Hey, I meant to ask. How is the line dancing going?"

"It's great—really fun," Ava lied, suddenly feeling uncomfortable. Keshawn had sent her the steps days ago, but she hadn't practiced at all. She looked at her phone.

"My dad's picking me up soon. Let me help you clean up," she offered.

The two girls put away the game and were sitting on the porch talking when Coach pulled up. He opened the window and waved.

"How you feeling, Kylie?" he asked.

"Great, Coach!" Kylie replied.

"I'll see you again soon," Ava promised.

Kylie grinned. "Monday. I'm allowed to go back to school!"

Ava climbed into the car and Coach started chatting, something about getting Chinese food because her mom was going to be working late in her pottery studio and he didn't feel like cooking—or eating Uncle Scott's cooking. But Ava wasn't paying much attention. She was trying to figure out the best way to practice that line dance.

I bet I can find videos on the computer, she thought. Yes, that would work. Alex did that all the time. She could look online and practice all weekend. She wasn't going to let Kylie down!

When her dad pulled into the driveway, Ava rushed out of the car.

"You're welcome!" Coach called after her.

She ran upstairs and shut the bedroom door behind her. Somewhere in her backpack she had printed out the dance steps that Keshawn had e-mailed her. She rummaged around and found the paper crumpled up underneath her notebook.

She smoothed it out and started to read.

```
Walk Forward
Grapevine Right
Grapevine Left
Step, Tap
Step, Tap
```

It might as well be written in Elvadoran, Ava thought. She flipped open her laptop and started typing, *Video of basic line dancing steps.*

"Yes!" Ava cried, as a list of videos popped up on the screen. There was one—four minutes long—"Basic Grapevine for Beginners."

"Perfect," Ava murmured, and she hit play. A

man and a woman wearing cowboy hats were facing the camera.

"To grapevine right, you need to start with your right foot," the woman began.

"Right foot," Ava repeated, and she started mirroring the steps on the screen. She stepped with her right foot, then put her left foot behind her right foot, and then . . . what were they doing?

"How did their feet end up there?" Ava asked out loud, and she started the video from the beginning.

She heard a whining, and Moxy pushed through her door, attracted by Ava's voice and the music. When she saw Ava dancing, she started to bark.

"Moxy, I am not some sheep you can order around!" Ava scolded. "Come on, I'm trying to dance!"

She walked back to the laptop and started the video again. Then she took a deep breath.

"Okay, start with a step to the right," she muttered as she tried to follow along.

"*Woof! Woof!*" Moxy barked.

Then Tommy stuck his head into the room. "Hey, Ave, Coach wants to know what you want to order—what are you doing? You look ridiculous."

Ava paused the video. "I am trying not to make a fool of myself!" she cried, flopping down on the bed.

"Uh-oh. Sounds like a crisis," Tommy said. "What's up?"

Ava launched into the story about how she had volunteered to take Kylie's place in the line dancing act.

"And I've realized I'm in way over my head. I can't do it!" she wailed.

"Come on, Ave, you know you can do anything you set your mind to," Tommy said, sitting on the bed next to her.

"Usually I can. But not this," Ava said. "It's like it's some weird Texas thing. I think you have to be Texan to do it."

"But you *are* Texan," Tommy said.

"Not really. We just moved here," Ava argued.

"I don't mean that. I mean Dad. He was born in Texas. So that makes us, like, authentic half Texans," Tommy pointed out. "In fact, you should probably ask Coach for help. He's a good dancer, and since he grew up here, I bet he knows how to line dance."

"Maybe," Ava said. She sat up and looked at the dancers paused on her computer screen.

"Right now, I don't think anybody could help turn me into a line dancer. Not even the Grand Wizard of Elvador."

Tommy looked at her. "You sure you're feeling okay?"

Ava sighed. "I'm fine. Just spent two hours playing a board game with Kylie."

Tommy stood up. "So, anyway, I'm supposed to ask you what you want from the Hungry Panda."

"Beef lo mein, please!" Ava replied, and then she flopped back down on the bed as Tommy left.

Moxy nudged Ava's feet with her nose.

"Woof! Woof!"

"Forget it, Moxy," Ava said. "I am done with dancing today!"

CHAPTER THIRTEEN

"Hey, Alex."

Corey slid in front of Alex as she took books out of her locker Monday morning.

"Oh, hey," Alex said, trying to sound casual and cool. Inside, she was doing a happy dance. She and Corey had only been bumping into each other since the Christmas party. She had been starting to wonder if he was avoiding her.

"So . . . ," Corey began, looking at her briefly before moving his gaze to his shoes. "I was wondering, do you want to hang out today? After school? With me?"

Alex let the words sink in. She restrained

herself from jumping up and down and saying, "Yes! Yes!"

"Yeah, sure," she replied. "Today works really well for me, actually, because I don't have a student council meeting and I don't have to do anything for the Variety Show and Ava doesn't have a basketball game," she babbled on.

Corey nodded when she finally stopped talking. "Cool. Maybe we can go to the park or something."

Alex smiled. "That would be nice!"

"Okay, so, um, I'll see you later," Corey said, a little awkwardly, and then he walked away.

Alex practically floated to her first-period class. Her good mood lasted exactly until third period, when, before class started, Mrs. Bridges motioned for Alex to come to her desk.

"Alex, I need to see you and Max back here after school," she said.

"But I—" Alex started to protest, but Mrs. Bridges held up her right hand.

"No excuses, please, Alex," the teacher said. "This is serious."

Alex sighed and nodded. "I'll be there."

She walked to her desk, passing Max along the way. He avoided her gaze, and Alex suddenly felt angry with him again. Thanks to him, she'd have to cancel hanging out with Corey. Why had she even bothered to help him in the first place?

When lunchtime came, Alex looked for Corey in the cafeteria. He and his friends were sitting at a different table from Alex's friends today, so she had to walk across the room to talk to him. He lit up with a smile when he saw her, which only made Alex feel more terrible about what she had to say.

"Corey, I'm sorry, but I actually can't hang out today," she said, and his smile quickly faded. "I totally forgot. I have to work on my social studies project with Max."

It was a lie, but just a little one. She didn't want to tell Corey about the cheating. That wouldn't be fair to Max, even though it was his fault they had to go talk to Mrs. Bridges after school.

"Oh," Corey said. "So, maybe some other time?"

"Yeah, definitely," Alex said.

As she walked over to her lunch table, she scolded herself. *I should have suggested another day!* she realized. Who knew when Corey would ask her again? Should she ask him?

"You look like a sad puppy," Emily said when Alex sat down next to her.

Alex looked over at Lindsey. She was busy talking with Charlotte, so Alex lowered her voice.

"I'm just disappointed, because Corey asked me to hang out today after school, and first I said yes, but then I had to cancel because I found out I have to do something else," she confided.

"Something better than hanging out with Corey?" Emily asked.

Alex sighed. "No. Definitely not better," she replied, and she didn't say anything more. She hadn't told anybody about Max's cheating—not even Ava. How could she explain that she was covering for a cheater? A cheater who was causing problems for her with Lindsey and Corey? She wasn't even sure why she was doing it.

Alex couldn't wait until the day was over and she could get the meeting with Max and Mrs. Bridges over with. She'd walk away with a warning, finish up the project with Max, and then she'd be done.

Max was already sitting in front of Mrs. Bridges's desk when Alex entered the room.

"Close the door behind you, please, Alex," the teacher instructed.

Alex obeyed and took a seat next to Max.

Mrs. Bridges took a deep breath. "So, I have

spoken with Principal Farmen, and she agrees with me that we need to have a meeting with your parents and consider putting you on academic probation if it happens again," she announced, and Alex gasped. That sounded a lot more serious than a warning!

"Cheating is not tolerated in this school," Mrs. Bridges said, looking at Max, and then she looked right at Alex. "Nor is helping someone else to cheat. Would you like to tell me what happened, Alex?"

Alex's mind was racing. There were more consequences to keeping quiet than she thought. If Alex told what she knew, Max could be in real trouble. If she didn't tell, then *she* could be in real trouble too. But she had a nagging feeling that whatever was happening with Max wasn't his fault. Even though he was totally messing things up for her, she didn't want to see him get in trouble.

"I don't know what happened," Alex said. "I did my homework on Monday night, by myself. If Max had the same answers as I did, I don't know why."

Which was all true, technically. She had a clue that Max had copied from her paper, but she hadn't actually witnessed it.

Mrs. Bridges kept her gaze locked on Alex. "So you have no idea how Max ended up with exactly the same answers as you."

Alex shook her head. It was getting harder to avoid the teacher's direct line of questioning.

"I copied from Alex's paper!" Max suddenly blurted out. "She didn't have anything to do with it and didn't know about it, I swear. She left her social studies folder on a table in the library, and when she walked away, I copied the homework answers."

Mrs. Bridges nodded as if that was what she'd been waiting to hear. "Thank you, Max. Alex, you may leave the room."

Alex quickly got up and left. This time she didn't linger outside the door—she didn't want to embarrass Max more by eavesdropping on his punishment.

Poor Max! she thought. But at least he had done the right thing and told the truth.

She walked down the hallway, wondering if Corey was at the park, and if it would be weird if she went to see if he was there. As she passed the auditorium, she heard country music playing. For a moment, she panicked. Was she supposed to meet Chloe and the others for a Variety Show meeting? She quickly checked her phone and saw that the next meeting wasn't until Thursday. It must just be an act using the auditorium for practice.

Curious, she slipped inside—and saw Ava, with the rest of the Toe the Line dancers, practicing their routine.

For a weird second, she wasn't sure if it was actually Ava out there—or herself! Her twin was having a hard time keeping up with the other dancers, and twice she bumped into the tall boy standing on her left. Which was all very Alex, and not very Ava at all. Although to Ava's credit, she wasn't tripping over her feet, like Alex would have.

What is up with her? Alex wondered, but the more she watched, the more she understood. It was a really complicated dance, more complicated than a cheerleading routine, even.

Then Alex remembered when Ava had talked to her about it, on the bus, and she had seemed a little unsure of herself—as though she were convincing herself to do it. If Alex hadn't been so wrapped up in all the Max and Lindsey drama, she might have given her sister some advice. Well, it was never too late. Alex waited until the practice was over.

"Good effort, Ava," Carly said, and Alex saw her sister cringe. She knew—and she knew that Ava knew—that "good effort" really meant, "You stink, but at least you're trying."

Alex waved Ava over when she climbed off the stage.

"Don't tell me you saw that," Ava said.

"Most of it," said Alex. "I can tell it's not easy."

"That's an understatement," Ava said with a sigh.

Then Alex had an idea. "Hey, you should ask Coach for help," she said. "He's a good dancer, and he grew up in Texas, so he probably knows how to line dance."

"That's what Tommy said," Ava told her.

"If both of your siblings are giving you the same advice, you should probably take it," Alex said.

Ava sighed. "Fine, I'll do it. I just wish I had never gotten into this in the first place!"

CHAPTER FOURTEEN

The next day at school Alex looked around anxiously for Max. She had no idea what had happened after he'd made his confession. Had he been suspended?

She finally saw him in the hallway on the way to social studies. His hair was a mess, there was a hole in the bottom of the T-shirt he was wearing, and his shoelaces were untied—so he looked pretty much the same as always. Alex couldn't tell if something bad had happened or not.

She wove through the crowd to talk to him, but Max saw her out of the corner of his eye and actually broke into a jog to avoid her. He obviously didn't want to speak to her. He quickly darted into class. When Alex entered, she saw that he had his notebook open and was pretending to study something very intently.

Alex tried to approach him again at lunchtime, as he walked out of the lunch line. But he made a sharp turn in the opposite direction, and Alex didn't follow. He was clearly avoiding her, embarrassed by what had happened.

But Alex really wanted to thank him. Copying her homework—that had been wrong. But telling the truth to keep Alex out of trouble—that was really brave. She didn't want Max to walk around thinking she was angry with him.

This is exactly like my Lindsey problem, Alex thought. *Max won't even talk to me!* Things were getting pretty frustrating.

Her twin noticed something was bothering Alex on the bus ride home.

"You've got that look on your face," Ava said. "And you've only told me three things that happened to you today, when normally at this point you would be up to ten things."

"Ha-ha," Alex said drily.

"You look like you're trying to figure out a problem," Ava said. "What's bugging you? The Lindsey thing?"

"Well, that, and then this thing happened with Max," Alex said, and she told her sister the whole story.

"Wow, Al, and you're not mad at him?" Ava asked.

Alex shook her head. "No. It was brave of him to tell the truth, and anyway, I think there's a reason he's cheating and it's not because he's lazy. Tommy thought there was something up with him too, when we gave him a ride home last week, and he thought I could figure it out. But I haven't been able to."

"Wait a minute. You know where he lives?" Ava asked.

Alex nodded. "Yes."

"So go over there and talk to him," Ava suggested. "He probably doesn't want to talk about it in school, where everybody can listen."

"Ave, that's a great idea!" Alex said. "He's in Magnolia Terrace. It's not that far. I'm going to ride my bike over there as soon as we get home. Thank you. That's great advice."

"Well, I owe you one," Ava said. "You and Tommy."

"What do you mean?" Alex asked.

"I'm finally going to take *your* advice," Ava

said. "I told Coach I needed help."

"You know, sometimes I wonder how people manage who don't have a twin," Alex remarked. "I mean, look at us. We're solving each other's problems!"

The bus came to a stop near the Sacketts' house.

"Not all our problems are solved yet!" Ava reminded her.

They got off the bus. Alex stuck with Ava's slow pace as they walked to the house, but as soon as they got inside, she bolted upstairs. She quickly changed out of the plaid skirt and white blouse she was wearing and into a T-shirt, leggings, and hoodie. Much better for bike riding.

Then she took her bike and helmet out of the garage, hopped on, and headed to Magnolia Terrace.

She didn't remember the house number, but she knew she just had to look for the white house with the overgrown grass. When she found it, she parked her bicycle by the front steps. Then she walked up and pressed the doorbell.

Through the door, she could hear the loud

wailing of a baby. Then a woman's voice yelled, "Max! Please get that!"

A minute passed, and nobody came to the door. Alex thought about pressing the doorbell again, but she felt bad. Things sounded pretty hectic inside.

Then there was the sound of feet, and the door opened. Max looked surprised to see her.

"Alex?" he asked.

"Um, can I please come in?" she asked. "I need to talk to you."

Max was too surprised to say no. He motioned for her to come in.

The sound of the baby's wails grew louder. Alex looked around and saw that the living room was a mess. There was a baby's playpen in the middle of the room and toys strewn about all over the floor. A basket of laundry spilled out onto the carpet.

A woman came out of the kitchen, talking into a phone. Her hair was swept up in a messy ponytail, she had a rag draped over her shoulder, and Alex could see the dark circles under her eyes from across the room. She didn't seem to notice Alex was there.

"Steven, you need to come home and help me

with this, please," she was saying. "I can't find her bottle, and she won't stop crying!"

Max nodded toward the staircase. "Downstairs. It's quieter."

He led her down a short flight of stairs into the family room. It was just as messy as the living room, but only a little quieter. Alex was starting to figure out why Max was always tired in school.

"Max, I just wanted to thank you," Alex blurted out. "For telling the truth. I understand why you didn't at first, but I'm really glad you did. And I hope you're not in too much trouble."

"I don't know yet," Max said. "I haven't gotten probation, but I think I might."

"Do your parents know?" Alex asked.

"I don't think so," Max said. "My dad is so busy that he never reads the e-mails from the school. And my stepmom hasn't said anything either."

"That's why you had to cheat, right?" Alex asked. "Because it's so chaotic here?"

A weary look swept over Max's face. "It's been crazy ever since the baby was born," he said. "Dad and Karen are like, freaking out, like they don't know what to do. The baby screams all night and I don't get any sleep. And when I ask Dad or Karen for help with homework, or to go to the library, they're always too busy."

"But I bet if they knew you were having trouble in school, they wouldn't be," Alex said. "I bet you got good grades before this, right?"

Max nodded. "How did you know?"

"Because you're smart," Alex told him. "You knew what the Fifth Amendment was without having to look it up, and you have an impressive vocabulary."

"Well, I have one of those word-a-day calendars," Max admitted.

"Me too!" said Alex, and they smiled at each other.

"You know, you should talk to your parents and teachers about what's going on," she said. "I'm sure they would understand."

"I probably should have done that already," Max said. "I just didn't want to make anything worse. But you're right—I don't want to fail out of middle school either! I'm just so tired, I'm not thinking straight."

Alex thought about how Ava had helped her solve this problem.

"Sometimes you just need a little help," she told him.

Ava sat perched on the couch at home, getting up every few minutes to see if Coach's car was pulling into the driveway. He was overseeing weight training at the high school this afternoon, and she couldn't wait for him to get home.

"So, you didn't say. What's this urgent problem you need my help with?" Coach asked when he finally walked in the door.

"Do you know how to line dance?" Ava asked.

Coach's green eyes started to twinkle. "Line dancing? That's your urgent problem?"

"It *is!*" Ava assured him. "I'm taking over for Kylie in this dance group. We're performing a big act at the Variety Show. I thought it would be easy, but I just can't get it—I'm dancing like Alex!"

Coach nodded gravely. "Okay, that is a problem. But you've come to the right man. I don't talk about it much, but I could do a mean line dance back in the day."

Ava handed him the sheet with the dance steps. "Do you know how to do all these?"

Coach took the sheet from her and grinned.

"Of course I do! Tell you what. Give me a minute and we'll get right on it. Do you have the song?"

"I can play it on my phone," Ava said.

"Then set up your phone in the speaker and we'll get started," Coach said. "First we'll go over the steps, and then we'll try them to the music."

"Thank you, thank you!" Ava said, hugging him.

Coach left the living room and returned wearing a cowboy hat. "Can't dance without the hat," he explained. Then he looked at the dance steps.

"All right, let's start with a grapevine," he said. "We'll start real slow. For a grapevine right, you step your right foot to the right."

He demonstrated, and Ava copied.

"Then you cross your left foot behind your right one," Coach instructed, making the move. Ava did the same.

"Then your right foot steps to the right, and your left foot meets the left side of the right foot," Coach explained, as he slowly did the steps.

"So that's how you do it!" Ava cried as she copied him. "Everyone does it so fast that I could never figure out how to do the ending."

"Let's do it a few more times," Coach suggested.

They practiced the grapevine right until Ava got the hang of it. Then Coach repeated the process with the rest of the moves: the heel dig, the pivot turn, the triple step, and the weave.

Once Ava had practiced each move, Coach pushed the coffee table out of the way to give them more space and told her to put the music on.

"Okay, now let's turn these moves into a dance!" he cried. "I'll call them out."

Ava nodded and took a breath. For the first time, she thought she might be able to do the dance after all. The strains of the song began.

"Walk forward!" Coach called out. "Grapevine right! Grapevine left! Step, tap! Step, tap! Pivot right!"

"Hey, I'm doing it!" Ava cried.

Just then Uncle Scott walked in the door. His face lit up when he saw what was going on in the living room.

"What, have you guys been line dancing in secret without me this whole time?" he asked. Without missing a beat, he stepped in line next to Coach and began to do the moves as Coach called them out.

"Heel dig, and clap!"

"Uncle Scott, you can line dance too?" Ava called out over the music.

"Hey, I've lived in Texas longer than your dad has," her uncle reminded her.

"Keep up, guys! Triple step!" Coach yelled.

The song ended, and Uncle Scott high-fived Ava. "Not bad, little lady," he said.

"I need to be better than not bad," Ava said. "I need to be great. Can we do it again?"

"I don't see why not," Coach said. "Set us up, Ava?"

Mrs. Sackett walked into the house, holding a bag of groceries. "Set up what?"

"We're teaching Ava how to line dance for the Variety Show," Coach replied.

"Hey, I want in on that!" Mrs. Sackett said. "Let me just get these groceries in the refrigerator."

"Is that what this is for? The Variety Show?" Uncle Scott asked.

Ava nodded. "Yes. It's next week."

"Good for you, Ava," Uncle Scott said. "I'm glad to see you're not letting your ankle get you down."

Ava looked down at her brace. She had been having so much fun that she had forgotten she was wearing it!

Mrs. Sackett rushed in. "Okay, let's do this!"

Ava was confused. "Mom, you're not from Texas."

"Your dad was big into line dancing when we met in college," she explained. "He used to take me to this country-and-western bar, and he taught me there. I think it was the only country-and-western bar in Massachusetts!"

Ava played the song again, and her mom lined up with her behind Coach and Uncle Scott. Coach called out the moves again. This time Ava felt like she knew what moves were coming next before Coach even called them out. It was finally getting easier!

Up from a nap, Moxy bounded into the living room and began to circle the dancers. At that moment, another Sackett got home—Alex, who had just returned from seeing Max.

She stopped cold when she saw the living room line dancing.

"Come join us, Alex!" Uncle Scott called out.

Alex shook her head. "No way. You don't know who you're asking."

When the song ended, everybody clapped.

"That was fun!" said Mrs. Sackett.

"I don't know what's happening to this family,"

Alex said. "Everyone's turning into Texans! Even Moxy."

"*Woof!*" Moxy barked at the sound of her name.

"Well, this Texan has an announcement to make," Uncle Scott said. "I got the new job!"

Mrs. Sackett let out a whoop, and Coach hugged his brother.

"It's about forty-five minutes away, over in Eagle Ridge," Uncle Scott informed them. "And I already found an apartment close by. I just signed the lease. I'll be moving out at the end of the month."

Mrs. Sackett almost let out another whoop, but contained herself. Ava and Alex looked at each other. Each twin knew what the other was thinking.

They both would be sad to see him go—but it would be nice to have just five Sacketts in the house again!

CHAPTER FIFTEEN

When Alex saw Max the next day, he didn't try to avoid her. In fact, he gave her a nervous smile and motioned for her to talk to him outside the social studies classroom.

"So, I talked to my parents last night," Max said. "They set up a meeting with Ms. Farmen today. If Alexa doesn't scream all the way through the meeting, it should be very productive."

"Wait, your baby sister's name is Alexa?" Alex asked.

"Yeah—oh wow, I didn't think of that," Max said. "That's pretty funny."

"I swear, I don't scream like that," Alex joked.

Max laughed. "Listen, I want to say thanks."

Alex wondered if she could keep her fingers crossed for Max all day but decided it would be much more effective to keep them crossed inside her head. She was so excited for Max that at lunch, she almost missed something significant.

Lindsey was walking past her, carrying her lunch tray, when her carton of milk fell off. Alex instinctively picked it up and handed it to her.

"Thanks, Alex," Lindsey said.

A few seconds later, it hit Alex. Lindsey had *talked* to her! After a week of the silent treatment! That meant there was hope.

Alex proceeded cautiously. Lindsey still treated her coolly during lunch. The girls started talking about their Dancing Divas outfits, and Alex listened in.

"I still say that the dresses with the sequins aren't 'Wild West' enough," Rosa said.

Emily started tapping her phone. "I still like the idea of wearing those cute vests we found, with a red pleated skirt."

"And cowboy boots," Annelise added.

Lindsey looked thoughtful. "Well, the red does go with the broken heart theme of the song."

As the girls talked about their costumes, Alex thought about the small breakthrough she'd had with Lindsey. It looked like Lindsey was slowly warming up to her—but how could Alex get her to defrost all the way?

Just another thing on my to-do list that I haven't crossed off yet, she thought. She still had to create the Variety Show program cover and finish her social studies project with Max.

So on Thursday, when Max approached her about working on the project together, she was relieved.

"I thought we could do it at my house," he said. "On Saturday, so we have time to get it all done."

"Your house?" Alex asked, thinking of the mess and the screaming baby. "Are you sure?"

Max smiled. "Yeah. Around ten?"

Alex nodded. "Okay."

She'd already finished the art for the Variety Show program, scanned it in, and added the text. At that afternoon's committee meeting, she showed it to everyone.

"Wow, that's even better than last year's," Kendall said, and Alex beamed with pride.

"Okay, so we have to get the finished program

to Mrs. Gusman by Monday morning so we can get copies printed in time for the show next Thursday," Chloe said. "I'm working on the final list, but we've got to decide the order of the acts." She took out a small pile of index cards with the name of an act on each one. Alex was impressed. Chloe was becoming almost as organized as Alex, and she was only a sixth grader.

Kendall started moving the cards around. "So, we always start out with a strong act and end with a strong act," she said. "We should definitely end with Toe the Line. They brought down the house last year."

Everyone agreed, and Alex realized what kind of pressure Ava must be under. She hoped the Sackett family line dancing lessons were helping.

"There are so many singing acts," Chloe said with a frown. "It would be nice to break them up with something. Oh well."

The committee meeting ended with everybody feeling confident that the show was going to go smoothly. Alex felt relieved to check off one item on her list.

On Saturday she got to Max's at ten in the morning. Once again, she could hear the sound of Alexa crying. She frowned. How were they supposed to work on this project?

This time, Max answered the door right away. Alex noticed that he was wearing a clean T-shirt, and he looked like he had gotten a good night's sleep.

Max's dad walked in, carrying the screaming baby. He had the same messy brown hair as his son.

"You must be Alex," he said. "Thanks for helping Max with his report."

"Well, you know, we're working on it together," Alex told him.

Mr. Beedle smiled. "That's awesome. Max, do you want to show her to the study while I give Alexa her bottle?"

"Sure," Max said, and Alex followed him back down to the family room. They walked through there all the way to the laundry room, and next to that was a small room with a desk and some bookshelves.

"We figured it out—this is the quietest place in the house," Max said. "Dad used to store stuff in here, but he turned it into a study for me."

"This is great," Alex said. "But what about the sleeping thing at night?"

"Dad had another great idea," he said. "He put this stuff on the wall between my room and Alexa's room. It's the same thing they use in recording studios to cut down the noise. It works pretty well."

Max moved over to the desk. "I've got my laptop down here, and it connects to the printer upstairs so we can print stuff out."

Alex sat in the chair across from him. "Great. I did a whole bunch of research last night."

As she emptied her backpack, the bookshelf behind Max caught her eyes. A black top hat sat on the highest shelf. The other shelves held books about magic: *101 Magic Tricks*, *Magic for Beginners*, and *Tips from the World's Greatest Magicians*. Next to the books were props that Alex deduced were probably used to perform magic tricks.

"Max, are you a magician?" Alex asked.

Max nodded. "Well, an amateur," he confessed. "I've been interested in it since I was a little kid. When Dad made this study for me, I figured this would be a good place to practice my tricks."

The gears inside Alex's brain were whirring.

"You've got to show me one!" she said.

Max seemed pleased to have an audience.

"All right," he said, and he stood up and then took some items off the shelf: a clear plastic cup, a paper tube, and a piece of paper.

"Let me ask you, young lady, would you pay a quarter to see a good magic trick?" he asked.

Alex played along. "Why, sure!" she said. She fished in her backpack and pulled out a quarter.

"Excellent!" he said, placing the paper on the table in front of him. "This paper mat insures that there is no trapdoor on top of this desk. Please place your quarter on the table and the trick will begin."

Alex obeyed. Max turned the plastic cup upside down. Then he placed the cardboard tube over it.

"Thank you for your donation, Alex. Now let's watch it disappear!"

He placed the tube and the clear plastic cup over the quarter. Then, with a flourish, he pulled up the tube. There was no quarter inside the plastic cup!

"Wow!" Alex cried.

"Because I like you, I'll tell you what," Max said. "This trick is on me."

He placed the tube back over the cup. Then he picked them both up—and there was the quarter, right where Alex had left it! He gave it to her and then gave a little bow.

Alex laughed. "How did you do it?"

Max wiggled his eyebrows. "A magician never tells his secrets. But that's a really basic trick. If I had more time to prepare, I could show you some better ones."

"You can show me next Thursday," Alex said. "At the Variety Show! We need a magic act."

Max looked unsure. "I thought about it, but won't everybody laugh at me? They already do, anyway."

"They'll laugh this time because you're funny," Alex promised. "Please? I'm on the committee, and we really need a good magic act. There are too many people singing pop songs."

Max thought about it. "I'll do it, on one condition," he said. "That you'll be my assistant!"

Alex was taken aback. "Me?"

"Sure," he said. "It'll be easy. You just have to hand me things when I ask you, stuff like that."

"And that's the only way you'll do it?" Alex asked.

Max nodded. "Yup."

Alex thought about it. Lindsey was finally warming up to her. How would she feel if Alex was in Max's act and not in the Dancing Divas? That wouldn't be easy to explain. But the show really needed a magic act, and it was so nice to see Max happy about something. . . .

Alex took out her phone. "Let me text Chloe."

Found a magic act for the Variety Show. Max Beedle. Too late to get him in the program?

Chloe texted back right away.

Nope—perfect! thanks! ☺

"Well, looks like we're in," Alex said, and then she decided to be honest with Max. "The only thing I'm worried about is that my friends wanted me to join their dancing act, and I turned them down. Partly because I was too busy, but mostly because I'm a terrible dancer!"

"Well, maybe you just need to explain it to them, and they'll understand," Max said. "That's the advice you gave me, and it worked. You have to find a way to show them how you feel."

Alex nodded. That had already worked with Emily, Rosa, Charlotte, and Annelise, but Lindsey still needed a little more sweetening—how could Alex show her that she really was sorry? She thought about the costumes the girls were discussing the other day and started to form an idea that might actually fix her problem.

"Okay, so project first, magic later!" Alex said.

They worked on the project all morning. Max's dad and stepmom ordered pizza for lunch, and after a quick meal, Alex and Max finished it up. Then Alex stayed until almost three o'clock, going over possible tricks with Max for the Variety Show.

"Well, I should get going," Alex said. "Thanks for having me over."

"Magic practice on Monday?" Max asked.

Alex mentally checked her schedule. "Sure!"

She stepped outside into a beautiful Texas afternoon, hopped on her bicycle, and headed home. She passed the park on the way, where a few boys were playing football—a pretty common sight in Ashland any day of the year. Then one of them called out her name.

"Alex!"

Corey jogged away from the game, and Alex stopped her bike so he could catch up.

"Hey, how did you know I was here?" he asked.

"I didn't," Alex replied. "I was just coming from Max's house."

Corey's face clouded, and Alex suddenly wished she had answered him differently.

"We finished our social studies project," she said quickly.

"Do you—do you—like Max?" Corey blurted out.

"No, of course not!" Alex protested. *I like you!* she wanted to say, but she wasn't brave enough. Instead an awkward silence hung between them.

"Okay, see you around," Corey said, and he ran back to join the game.

Alex was mortified. Did Corey really think she liked Max? Then what would he think when they performed together in the Variety Show?

The thought worried her the whole ride home. As she put her bicycle away, Ava walked out the front door, eating an apple.

"Where've you been?" she asked.

"Over at Max's house," Alex answered, and then she explained what had happened.

"A magic act?" Ava repeated.

Alex nodded. "Yes. It's really funny and cute. And I just have to hand him things and smile."

Ava laughed. "I can't wait to see *you* being someone's assistant."

"So it looks like the Sackett twins will both be appearing in the Variety Show," Alex said with a grin. "The amazing performing Sackett twins!"

"Let's just hope we're not the amazing falling-on-our-faces Sackett twins!" Ava joked.

"I've seen you dancing," Alex said. "You're getting better! You're not going to fall on your face."

Ava looked down at her brace. "I hope not!"

On Tuesday, Ava couldn't concentrate on anything in her seventh-period class. She kept looking at the clock, willing the big hand to move faster. Finally it hit two o'clock, and an announcement came over the classroom speaker.

"Ava Sackett, please report to the office."

Ava contained a whoop of joy and nodded to her teacher as she hurried out of the room. In the office, she found her mom waiting for her.

"Ready, Ave?" she asked.

"I've been ready since I woke up!" Ava replied.

Mrs. Gusman, the school secretary, looked up

from her desk with an amused expression.

"I've never seen a student so happy about a doctor's visit before," she said.

"I'm hoping for some good news," Ava said, holding out her leg to show her brace.

Mrs. Gusman nodded. "Good luck, then, Ava."

Ava was bouncing in the seat on the whole drive to see Dr. Rodriguez. In the waiting room, she bounced her left leg up and down the whole time. Finally she got called into his office.

"So Ava, how's the ankle doing?" he asked, as she hopped up onto the exam table.

"Great! Really great!" she replied enthusiastically. "Really, really great!"

The doctor laughed. "Okay, I get the picture," he said. He removed the brace and examined her ankle, gently moving it up and down.

"Let me see you walk on it without the brace," he instructed.

Ava obeyed—her ankle didn't hurt at all anymore! It felt as good as new.

Dr. Rodriguez nodded. "That does look pretty great. I'd like you to keep wearing the brace for three more weeks, but you can go back to your normal physical activity."

"Like playing basketball?" Ava asked.

"Yes, like playing basketball," the doctor replied.

"Woo-hoo!" Ava cheered, jumping up.

"How about you get the brace back on before you do that?" Dr. Rodriguez suggested.

"What? Oh, sure," Ava said, quickly strapping on the brace.

She practically skipped out of the office ahead of her mother, she was so happy.

"Mom, I can go to practice tonight, right?" Ava asked.

"If Dr. Rodriguez said so, then yes," Mrs. Sackett replied.

"Woo-hoo!" Ava cheered again.

Ava's mom shook her head and chuckled. "Trust me, I'm as happy as you are that you can play basketball again."

The car approached the park on the way to the Sacketts' house, and Ava could see Jack shooting hoops by himself. His backpack was thrown off to the side—he must have stopped at the park on the way home from school. Ava looked at her mom—and her look said everything.

Mrs. Sackett pulled the car over. "One hour, Ava. Then you need to get homework done before tonight's practice. Got it?"

"Got it!" Ava said. "Thank you!"

She ran—for the first time in three weeks—to the basketball court.

"Hey! Over here!" she called out.

Jack turned toward her and grinned. Then he passed her the ball. Ava dribbled it up to the basket, then jumped up for a layup shot. The ball bounced off the backboard into the net.

"Good to have you back," Jack said.

CHAPTER SIXTEEN

"Okay, everybody! Acts one through five, please stay backstage. Acts six through twenty, we need you to wait in the music room!" Alex yelled over the hubbub of voices backstage.

It was the night of the Variety Show—thirty minutes before the curtain opened, to be exact— and Alex was running around backstage with a clipboard, just as Emily had predicted.

"Okay, I've got the first five here!" Chloe called out.

"Great!" Alex replied. "I'm going to the music room."

Alex headed there to organize the remaining acts—but she was on a mission, too. Her plan to win Lindsey back wouldn't succeed if Alex didn't find her friends, fast.

Chaos greeted her inside the music room, as the performing students talked excitedly, warmed up their voices, practiced their acts, and put the finishing touches on their costumes. Alex spotted Ava first, going over the line dance with Toe the Line. Her sister wore a cowboy boot on her left foot and a sneaker on her right foot with the brace.

Alex waved at her twin, but Ava was concentrating hard on the moves and didn't notice.

Next, Alex passed by Max. She was surprised to see that he had cleaned up nicely for the event. He wore a white shirt tucked into black pants, and a black skinny tie. Gel slicked back his normally messy hair. He looked up from his box of props as Alex walked by and gave her a thumbs-up.

When Max asked her to be his assistant, she had worried that she might have to wear some silly costume. But Max told her to just stick to black and white, so she'd worn a short black skirt with a white blouse, black tights, and black flats. She and Max would look perfect together onstage.

That was a good thing and a bad one too. She liked Max but she didn't *like* him—not the way she liked Corey. And she knew Corey was definitely going to think she might *like* Max once he saw them onstage together. She had tried to grab a minute with Corey to talk with him about it, but there never was a right time at school, and she'd been busy every day after school prepping for the show.

Alex pushed the worry aside. She had bigger things to take care of first! She spotted the Dancing Divas in a corner and rushed up to them.

"Hey, you guys look great!" she said. Each of her friends wore a short red pleated skirt, a white T-shirt, and a brown vest embroidered with red hearts.

"When are we on, Alex?" Emily asked, nervously tugging on the end of her skirt.

"You're number ten," Alex told them. "I'll come get you in plenty of time, don't worry."

Then Alex took a small drawstring pouch off her shoulder. "I made something for you guys," she said.

She pulled out five thin elastic red headbands. On each one, Alex had sewn a red felt heart that she'd embroidered with zigzag lines in black thread.

"Broken heart headbands, to go with the song," Alex said.

"Oh, Alex, they're perfect!" Rosa gushed, grabbing one, and each of the girls took one, even Lindsey.

"So cool," Emily said. "We should go put these on in the restroom, so we can see how they look."

"I wanted to do something for you—all of you—to apologize," Alex explained. "I honestly think your dance is really cute. And the main reason I didn't want to do it is because I can't dance. I mean, I seriously can't!"

Emily nodded. "I know. I've seen you," she teased.

"So, the show needed a magic act, and I'm helping Max Beedle onstage," Alex said. "I hope you all understand. All I have to do is hand him things. It's so much easier than dancing."

Then she looked at Lindsey. "I know you don't like him. But I really think he's nice, and he didn't mean to hurt your feelings. And you're my friend first, Lindsey, always."

Lindsey sighed and looked down at the

headband. "I know. I'm sorry for not talking to you, and I'm sorry if I was mean to Max. He's actually not so bad."

"Thanks," Alex said, and she remembered why she was friends with Lindsey in the first place. Under that armor, she could be really nice.

"Group hug!" Annelise called out, and the girls converged on one another, giggling.

"All right, I've got to get backstage," Alex said, looking at her watch. "The show's starting soon. You guys are going to be great!"

Alex could feel the excitement in the air once she got backstage. The lights in the auditorium had dimmed, and Ms. Farmen walked onstage under the glow of a spotlight.

"Welcome, everyone, to the Ashland Middle School Variety Show!" she announced. For a small woman, she had a commanding voice, Alex had always thought. "This year's theme is the Wild West, and I'm sure we're all in for a wild time tonight. So sit back and enjoy the show!"

Ms. Farmen walked offstage as the curtain opened behind her. Jack and Spencer stood there with their backs to the audience. Then hip-hop music blared through the speakers and they came to life, launching into their dance. The audience went crazy.

Backstage, Chloe motioned to a girl in a sparkly blue dress.

"Number two, you're up next!" she said. Then she nodded to Alex. "Let's get number six in here."

Alex ran to the music room to get the next act. Only five acts were backstage at a time. When one act went onstage, Alex would bring another group backstage to wait. The committee had planned out the show like a well-oiled machine, and she was loving it. Plus, she got to catch a glimpse of all the performances.

After Billy Scarbek balanced a chair, a broom, and a hockey stick on his nose, all to thunderous applause, it was the Dancing Divas' turn. Alex had to admit that they all looked supercute, and the headbands just made them even more so.

Alex watched her friends as the music played on stage.

"... *nothing hurts more than a broken heart ...*"

She still thought the act was a little silly, but she would never let her friends know that. They did move in perfect time and looked adorable besides. By the time they had traced their last heart shape in the air with their fingers, the crowd was in love with them.

Alex ran back to bring act number sixteen into the waiting area, and when she returned, she heard Chloe call her name.

"Alex! Max! You're up next!"

Alex suddenly felt her palms get sweaty. Speaking in front of people didn't normally make her nervous, but this was different. This was a magic act! What if it was terrible? What if she made a mistake?

"Come on," Max said, pushing his cart of props onto the stage.

Alex followed him, squinting under the bright lights.

"Hello, everyone. I am Max the Magician, and this is my lovely assistant, Alex!"

Alex waved to the audience, as they had practiced, and was relieved to hear the crowd applaud.

"Alex, my hat, please," Max said, and Alex's nerves left her and they began their routine. Alex had gone over the moves so many times she knew them by heart.

Four minutes later, after Max had made a stuffed rabbit appear and disappear and pulled an impossibly long string of colorful scarves out of Ms. Farmen's pocket, the act was over. Applause and cheers followed Max and Alex offstage.

"Wow, guys, that was so cool!" said Emily, who had stayed backstage with the Dancing Divas to watch the magic act.

"Yeah, and you were pretty funny, Max," Charlotte added, and Max blushed.

Chloe handed Alex her clipboard. "Nice job. Can you get me number eighteen, please?"

Alex headed for the music room, relieved to be an organizer again instead of a magician's assistant.

What did Corey think of that? she wondered, but that was a problem for another day.

Two country ballads, three jazz dancers, and one opera singer later, it was time for the final act: Toe the Line. The crowd roared when the dancers came out. Alex anxiously watched, hoping everything would go okay for Ava.

Onstage, Ava looked out at the crowd. There, in the front row with her leg sticking out, was Kylie.

"Go, Ava!" Kylie cheered, just as she had at Ava's basketball game.

All right, Ava, you can do this! Ava told herself. *For Kylie!*

The music started, and Ava focused with all her might. Carly wouldn't be calling out the steps during the performance. But that was okay, because she had practiced so much that the steps were burned in her memory.

Walk forward!

Grapevine right!

Grapevine left!

Step, tap!

Step, tap!

Pivot right!

The song was over before Ava knew it, and the crowd erupted in applause and cheers. The Toe the Line dancers bowed and then marched off the stage.

"Ava, you did it!" Alex cheered, running up to hug her sister.

"Yeah, I did," Ava said, as if she didn't quite believe it herself.

"Great job, everybody!" Kendall called out. "Some of you might know that we have a Variety Show tradition every year. Ice cream at Rookie's!"

All the performers and crew let out a cheer.

"I think I sweat at least two gallons tonight," Alex confided in her sister. "Some ice cream would hit the spot right now."

Mrs. Sackett and Coach gave them big hugs as the girls came out from backstage, then dropped them off at Rookie's, which was decorated to look like an old-fashioned ice cream parlor. There was a long counter with stools in front of it, and round metal tables with padded chairs.

Inside, the place was packed. Alex spotted the Dancing Divas crowded around a small table and waved. Then Ava tapped her.

"Come say hi to Kylie with me," she said, pointing.

Kylie and Owen were sitting around a table with two empty chairs, and Kylie was motioning for them to come over.

"One of the benefits of a broken leg," Kylie said, when they arrived. "It's easy to get a table."

"Why don't you guys tell me what you want, and I'll place the order," Owen said.

"Chocolate shake, please," said Ava.

"Vanilla shake, please," said Alex at the same time.

Kylie laughed. "That's so perfect. You guys are,

like, the same but different. Both milk shakes, but different flavors."

"Wow, that is deep, Kylie," Ava teased.

"I think Kylie's right," Alex said thoughtfully. "We are alike in some ways, but in many ways we're different."

"Yeah, I guess so," her sister agreed.

Owen came back. "They'll bring the stuff to our table," he said. Then he turned to Kylie. "Did you see that video I posted for you? It's instructions for making a Stellar Warrior costume. Super cool."

Kylie picked up her phone. "No way! I've got to see that."

Soon the two of them were engrossed in the video. Ava turned to her sister.

"Do you think we're more alike, or more different?" she asked.

Alex looked thoughtful. "Well, different, I guess, but alike in the more important ways."

"Like what?" Ava asked.

"Like, we both tried new things tonight," Alex said. "Would you have believed me if I told you a year ago that you were going to be onstage in a Texas Variety Show doing a traditional Texas dance, and killing it?"

Ava laughed and shook her head. "No way. I would have thought you were crazy."

"And who would have ever thought I would be a magician's assistant?" Alex said. "So we're both brave. And that's a pretty important way we're alike."

"And don't forget talented," Ava said. "I mean, who knew I could line dance or you could do magic?"

"Exactly," said Ava. "I wonder what other hidden talents we'll discover here in Texas?"

A server arrived and placed their ice cream orders on the table. Ava reached for her milk shake.

"How about a talent for drinking milk shakes really fast?" Ava asked.

Alex laughed as her sister slurped down her milk shake. Then she took a long, slow sip of her own.

Belle Payton isn't a twin herself, but she does have twin brothers! She spent much of her childhood in the bleachers reading—er, cheering them on—at their football games. Though she left the South long ago to become a children's book editor in New York City, Belle still drinks approximately a gallon of sweet tea a week and loves treating her friends to her famous homemade mac-and-cheese. Belle is the author of many books for children and tweens, and is currently having a blast writing two sides to each It Takes Two story.

IT TAKES TWO

More books about Alex and Ava?
That's TWO good to be true!

Available at your favorite store!